D1797792

Natalie Tereshchenko - The Other Side
Copyright © 2014 by Elizabeth Audrey Mills
Published by Elizabeth Audrey Mil's

ISBN: 978-1497300194

This is a work of fiction. Names, characters, places, brands,
media, and incidents are either the product of the author's
imagination or are used fictitiously.

Written using yWriter by Spacejock Sof-ware
Plume-Creator by Cyril Jacquet
and LibreOffice by The Document Foundation

Cover by The Cover Collection

Email: elizabeth@itsliz.net
Website: www.itsliz.net

"The story of Natalie Tereshchenko is the story of the Russian people."

My thanks go to Jane Austen and Bernadine Evaristo for pointing the way, to Gabrielle Kimm for showing how it should be done, to Sandra Goose and Aubree Lane for spotting those inevitable little typing errors and plot-holes in my drafts, to my friends in Facebook and the real world for their encouragement, and to my hubby, Douglas, for his patience and advice.

Dedicated with love to my daughter, Tina.

Overture

~ *Moscow, Saturday 27 July 1918* ~

A figure loomed in the half-light at the edge of the officer's vision. "Someone's coming out of the front doors, Sir," it said.

Captain Sergeyev looked up from the chart he was studying by the glow of a flash-light, and saw the silhouette of Sergeant Korovin saluting him. Vaguely returning the salute, he turned to look at the convent. A small, grey shape was visible at the top of the steps, but at this distance, in the long shadows of dawn, he was unable to see any detail.

"Turn on the searchlights, and tell your men to be ready," he instructed, grabbing his binoculars and stepping out from his position of concealment behind the truck to get a better look.

The sergeant shouted his orders, and there was a clatter of weapons being armed, followed by a sharp thud as the nearest searchlight flared, quickly repeated by the other two. The three beams stabbed the darkness, wavering for a moment before meeting on the church front.

Sergeyev raised his binoculars to examine the figure suddenly illuminated at their convergence, and was surprised at what he saw. Many sights had passed through those brown eyes, including some that he would like to forget, but never anything like this. A skinny young woman was standing at the top of the church steps, her arms raised at her sides as though in welcome, and, as far as he could see, she was completely naked.

"Hold your fire," he shouted over his shoulder as he

began to stride briskly towards the diminutive, white figure, then ducked as one nervous soldier jerked the trigger of his rifle, sending a shot whistling close past his head. He turned back to glare at his sergeant. "Get that man's name," he spat.

Sergeant Korovin saluted, and the Captain resumed his march to where the figure was now lying on slabs at the top of the wide, stone steps of the convent.

Sergeyev was a man of action. In February 1917 he had led his men of the Volynsky regiment out from their barracks in Petrograd to join the revolution. These brave Cossacks, who had faced death for years fighting for the Tzar against Germany, found the command to open fire on unarmed civilians an affront to even their hardened souls. Instead, they took their guns and crossed the divide to march alongside the men and women from the factories. Now, a year-and-a-half later, he commanded those same soldiers in Moscow, in the name of the new communist government.

"Who the hell are you?" he asked the inert form when he reached her, removing his jacket and, kneeling beside her, laying it over her body, covering her nakedness. She looked like a child ~ pale-skinned, her pretty face at rest, a trickle of blood running across her brow from a furrow close to her hairline, to where it flowed into her long hair that lay like a cushion under her head, hair and blood merging in a dark pool. One hand was raised to her chest, touching a pendant that hung by a fine silver chain that glinted at her neck. As though to dramatise the moment, he heard, floating on the morning air, the ethereal voices of the nuns inside the convent, singing their prayers.

Standing up, he turned back to the line of soldiers and gestured to his sergeant to join him.

"Take her to the hospital, Yuri," he said, when the man

arrived, "and stay with her until she regains consciousness. Find out who she is."

"Yes, sir," answered Korovin, stooping to gently pick up the limp body.

"And bring my jacket back," Sergeyev added, gruffly.

The sergeant grinned, and the Captain watched him depart, then turned, hands on hips, to face the church, silently debating his next move. All his plans were now void.

"What a mess!" he said, shaking his head.

Then, a decision made, he strode up to the doors, threw them open, and entered.

Chapter 1

~ Heaven Delayed ~

My arrival in heaven was disappointing, to say the least. As consciousness returned, I was surprised to find that the journey there was much bumpier than I had expected ... and I had a headache.

I was sure I must be dead ~ fifty bullets (give or take a few) should have made certain of that. But, when I opened my eyes, I saw that heaven appeared to be remarkably like the place I had just left. Trees, lamp-posts and very ordinary buildings were flitting past, starkly lit by the low sun against a deep blue sky. I turned my head a little to take in my surroundings, and winced as a sharp stab of pain shot between my temples. I had been aware of the hurt nestling like a hiding cat behind my forehead ~ lurking, quietly pulsing, pressing against my eye sockets ~ but with the slight movement it leapt out and savaged me. I closed my eyes again, submitting to the agony.

When it subsided again, and I reopened my eyes, I saw, close to my face, a male chest in soldier's uniform, and, above it, the chin of a man, his image blurred by the constant bouncing. I could hear the roar of a motor car engine, and smell the hot-oil aroma of its exhaust.

The man became aware that I had woken. "Hello, miss. Sorry it's so rough," he said, kindly, in a voice I thought I vaguely recognised.

At that moment, I realised that I could feel the cold leather of the car seat against the skin of my back. Not only was I lying with my head in the lap of a strange man, in the back of a strange vehicle, but also, except for the

5

loose cover of a rough army jacket draped over me, I was completely naked. A memory flashed of my recent actions, and a little squeal of panic rose from my throat.

The man's expression became concerned. "Please do not be afraid," he said, quickly. "I will not harm you. I am taking you to hospital, you have been hurt."

I began to remember details ... Sacha and my mother, badgering me to be the new Tsarina, to front the Whites' counter-revolution. Then a spotlight ... no, three ... and many hidden soldiers ... the first gunshot. If I was not dead, then I must surely be gravely injured. I tried to use my hands to feel for wounds in my body, but each movement caused the jacket to slip a little, so I stopped, my eyes wide with desperation, grasping at the fabric to hold it over me.

The man smiled, looking down at me kindly, and rearranging the scant covering a little for me. His young face was oddly familiar, like seeing a familiar landscape from a different angle.

"You are not badly hurt," he said reassuringly, just a graze on your head."

"A graze!" I spluttered. "Are they all such terrible shots in the new army?"

He laughed. "Only one man actually fired his gun, and he is to be reprimanded."

"But I thought you had come to kill me," I said, puzzled.

"No," he grinned. "Why would we want to do that?"

It was then that I saw his full face clearly for the first time, and the pieces fell together.

"Yuri?" I cried. Yuri had been a good friend to me, a year earlier, when I was carted off into exile in the company of the royal family.

He nodded. "I could not believe it when I saw you lying

6

on the steps of the convent," he said, "and I dared not mention anything to the captain."

I was about to reply, but before either of us could say any more the vehicle swerved right and left ~ sending pain stabbing again through my head ~ and screeched to a halt.

"We are at the hospital," Yuri announced. "Just relax, the doctors will check you over."

The door above my head was opened by another soldier, and Yuri carefully and effortlessly carried me into the outside world, holding the jacket in place to make sure that I was at least sem-decently covered. I felt air around parts of my body that should not be exposed, and his hands on skin that only Max had touched before. I wanted to curl up and die with shame.

* * *

Later, when the doctors had finished with me, and I had been transferred onto a ward 'for observation' Yuri came to my bedside. He had gained weight since I last saw him ~ it suited him, he looked ... content and healthy. His hair was cut close to his scalp, and he was neatly shaved. He wore the uniform of a sergeant comfortably, as though he had held the rank all his life, and he carried a soft cap rolled up in his hand.

"Well," he said as he brought a chair to my bedside and sat beside me, "this is a strange moment. How do you feel?"

"Better than I expected," I replied, smiling. "And more respectably dressed. You have been promoted, I see."

I had first known Yuri when he was just a private, guarding the royal family at Alexander Palace and on the train when we went into exile. At a time when feelings against the Tsar and Empress were running high, and the soldiers assigned to protect them were, for the most part, resentful and hostile, he was kind and thoughtful. It was not that he was a supporter of the monarchy, I knew that he was as critical as anyone about the way they had exploited the people and mismanaged the country's affairs, but his intelligence and professionalism rose to suppress any dislike he held for them and to conduct himself with dignity.

"Yes," he grinned, twisting his arm to look at the stripes on his sleeve. "Sergeant Korovin of the Red Army; they know a good man when they see one." He laughed. "But what a shock to see you again, and in such strange circumstances. I'm glad it was me with the captain, and of course I am happy to see you again, but I have been instructed to report back to him with details of why you did such a strange and foolish thing."

I knew that I was safe with Yuri, but I did not want to reveal too much. The fact that I was still alive was puzzling, and I needed to learn more about the situation. I deflected his question with one of my own:

"Why were you all gathered outside the church?" I asked, side-stepping an explanation that would be difficult.

For a moment, it looked as though he was not going to answer. His eyes wandered vaguely off towards the opposite side of the ward, and he stared briefly at the space in between, deep in thought. Then, decisively, he returned his attention to me. "I suppose I can tell you," he answered, quietly, "as our mission is now completed. We were there to close the convent and arrest the Abbess, Elizabeth Feodorovna. There is a new law that all churches are to become property of the State."

'They were not there for me!' I thought. *'Apart from Yuri they don't even know who I am!'*

"Why? What has she done?" I asked, my mind racing.

"It is not so much that she has done anything, but that

8

she is the sister of Alexandra, the former Empress," he replied. "Did you not know that?"

"I knew," I told him. "I was shocked when I met her ~ the likeness was uncanny. But I don't think many of the others were aware; we referred to her only as Mother Superior." I hesitated. "Do you know that the whole royal family was murdered?"

"I had heard a rumour; though nothing official, of course."

"Everyone," I told him, bluntly. "The children, Ivan, Doctor Botkin, even poor Alexei Trupp!" I felt tears welling up as I remembered them all.

He reached out a hand and touched mine, a gesture of friendship and sympathy. "Why did they spare you?" he asked, puzzled.

Without thinking, I shook my head, then regretted it as pain surged across my temples and nausea swept through me. With a grunt, I closed my eyes and took a slow breath to steady myself; I felt his hand squeeze mine reassuringly. After a while I was able to answer him:

"They didn't, I was able to escape with the help of one of the guards."

I told him about Max and our flight from the murdering Avadeyev and his men. "With the help of the nuns, I became sister Ephraimia," I told him, "and came with them from Nizhny Novgorod to the convent on a pilgrimage. The plan is to rejoin Max here in a few days, then continue together to England, somehow."

"So, if you were in hiding, why did you walk out through the front doors of the church wearing nothing but the skin you were born in?" he probed, a slight smile on his lips.

A natural question, and difficult to answer. I certainly could not admit the real reason, the complicated decision to end my own life ~ I would not burden my friend with knowledge of my royal blood ~ but a credible excuse eluded me. It was a most irrational thing for any woman to do, if you did not know the agonising process by which I had reached that conclusion. As I thought about it, I felt my face flush and I looked down at my hands. "I am very embarrassed," I whispered. "Will you just accept my assurance that it is not something I have ever done before, and have no intention of ever doing again?" I looked up into his eyes, which were studying my face, kindly. Yuri was a good man, a family man; I could imagine him with his children and adoring wife.

"You could have been killed," he admonished, berating me with a fierce expression. Then his face broke into a grin. "I am happy to see you again, and you don't have to explain anything to me, but I have to tell my commanding officer something, and he will not be easily misled. What do you want me to tell him? I will say whatever you wish, but he will want to know your full name, at least, and some kind of explanation."

"Will you tell him that I have no memory of whatever events led me to be there? Amnesia from the bullet wound. If he doesn't accept that, I will have to try something else. As for my identity, I cannot use my real name. If Avadeyev is still searching for me, he is looking for Natalie Tereshchenko, and will have circulated my name to every town in western Russia. The false papers that I have been using are all in my room at the convent,"

"I may be able to get them for you. What was your adopted surname?"

"Thank you; it was Nestorova ~ Ephraimia Nestorova. I think I should keep that identity, as it gives me a past, albeit a fake one. My real identity must never come out." I stopped and wagged a finger, smiling, but it was an important point I had to make. "From now on, you must remember to call me Mia."

He pursed his lips, clearly suppressing a grin. "That will not be easy at first. But I will practise." He stood and scooped up his cap and the jacket in which I had arrived at the hospital. "I must go now and return the captain's jacket. I will report to him that you cannot remember anything about the incident. If I can get your papers, I will bring them here for you." He stood and leaned over to kiss my cheek. "I am very pleased to see you again."

"Me too," I smiled, holding him close.

Chapter 2

~ *Sacha* ~

I was not alone for long after he departed, for as I began to nod off I received another visitor, my friend Sacha. Her face was set in a grim expression; she was clearly agitated. "What on earth are you playing at?" she demanded, vehemently, as soon as she was seated beside my bed.

We had met when she stayed briefly at Alexander palace, a lifetime ago, when our troubles were just beginning, and we had immediately formed a bond. Then our fates sent us in opposite directions, and I had not seen her since, until her surprise visit at the convent yesterday (was it really only yesterday?) with my mother.

"Thank you for your concern," I replied caustically, "I'm not too bad, considering that a bullet bounced off my skull this morning. I just have concussion and a raging headache; nothing to worry about."

"Well you have no-one to blame but yourself," she said, glaring at me.

"I know that, but why are you so angry?" I asked, surprised at the force of her response.

"I just don't understand why you did it," she replied. "Getting yourself shot like that." Then, seeing that I was about to speak, she continued, pointing an accusing finger at me: "And don't tell me it wasn't deliberate."

Chastened, I chose not to answer, but instead asked a question of my own; this deflection technique was becoming part of my repertoire. "How did you find out I am here?"

She eyed me, piercingly, aware that I was holding out.

"Before the Abbess Elizabeth was arrested, she managed to send one of the nuns with a message for your mother, who was staying overnight with us, telling her what had happened."

My mother, Sofiya, was the cause of my predicament. When she was much younger, she had an affair with one of the Tsar's brothers, and I was the result of their liaison. Not only had that placed me with the royal family through their trials, but it had also burdened me with a secret link to the monarchy. Now she saw an opportunity to cash in on it; she wanted me to exploit my half-royal blood and become a figurehead for the White resistance movement.

"Why does she have to interfere in my life?" I asked, angrily. "She managed to stay out of it for sixteen years. Why can she not just leave me alone now?"

"Because she wants something better for you," Sacha said, trying to sound reasonable, conciliatory.

"No," I responded hotly, "she wants a good life for herself, and would see me dead while she schemes and manoeuvres to get it. Is she here with you now?" I looked towards the door, half expecting to see her lurking there. "If she is, I do not want to see her. Tell her I am too weak for visitors. No, tell her I never want to see her again."

Sacha shook her head. "She caught the train back to Petrograd an hour ago. That's one reason why I came here. The convent is closed, boarded up, you can't return there, but you are welcome to stay with my mother and me until you can find somewhere of your own."

It was a kind gesture, and I smiled gratefully, as I also relaxed in the knowledge that Sofiya was not there. "Thank you, I have been worrying about that since Yuri told me what is happening."

I paused for a moment, and reached out my hand to her. She took it and held it tightly with both of her own, returning my smile.

"Sacha," I continued, "I know you think Sofiya's plan would be good for me, but it's not what I want. I thought hard and long before stepping out of the church, it was not an easy decision to take. And yes, I knew the soldiers were there."

"I knew I was right!" she exclaimed, smiling tensely with satisfaction. "What exactly was going on in that strange place between your ears?"

I grinned; this was more like my old friend Sacha, the one I remembered from our brief time together at Alexander Palace. I stuck out my tongue, and she laughed and squeezed my hand.

"I was at the top of the bell-tower," I explained, "and saw the soldiers moving into position. I was sure they had to be there for me, perhaps alerted by my mother's visit: it didn't cross my mind that it could have been the Abbess Elizabeth they wanted. I decided that, if I was going to die, it would be on my terms, not trying to scuttle away like a mouse startled by the light. That's why I took off my robes; I didn't want them to kill a nun, or be restrained from shooting because they thought I was a nun."

"I think you were very brave, if misguided. But why did you want to die? It was a shock when I heard what you had done, especially after we had been talking about the future the previous day."

"It was the thought of the future we discussed that repelled me, Sacha. I cannot be Tsarina, it's not in me. I believe that people should be free to choose their own destiny, not have it foisted on them by some-one who knows nothing of their lives ~ who, in fact, owns them, like slaves. My intention was that the royal line should end with my death, never to rise again. It wasn't really bravery, more like a coward's way out of a difficult situation."

She shook her head. "I can't understand your thinking. You could have a fine life, and perhaps bring about changes for the better in Russia."

"It would be a false life, Sacha; against all my principles."

"Well, it's your choice, Natalie dear. What will you do next?"

"You have to remember to always call me Mia," I admonished. "There must be no slip-ups."

"Oh yes, Mia," she said thoughtfully, looking at me. "I suppose I can get used to that."

"As for what to do next," I continued, "that is a hard question to answer. It is a great help that I can stay with you until Max arrives. I hope that then we will be able to continue our escape. Somehow we have to get to England."

* * *

Sacha left, promising to return the next morning, and the rest of the day passed slowly. Lunch was served, soup and bread, then cleared away. I dozed for a while ~ my wound sent me a twinge occasionally, lest I should forget it, but I didn't feel too bad, and was enjoying my enforced rest.

Late in the afternoon, Yuri brought me a small bundle containing my identification papers, my robes and shoes. "Is this really all you have, now?" he asked, setting them on the narrow table between my bed and the next.

"Yes, that's it," I said. "What little else I own was left behind in Nizhny, including my diaries."

"Ah, your diaries, yes. You will need them if you are to write your book."

I smiled, wanly. "I don't suppose I will ever see them again, and perhaps that is just as well. Can you tell me about the Abbess, Yuri? What is to happen to her? Will she be murdered, like the rest of the family?"

He shook his head. "She is being held under arrest for the time being, but will probably be deported to Germany, her home country."

I stared across the room for a while, the beds arranged along the green-painted walls in neat rows, with white sheets and grey blankets. The people in them anonymous, like extras in a movie ~ a doctor attending one, a nurse drawing screens around another.

My memories flashed past like the pages of a book, flipped by phantom fingers. Images of the events that had brought me to this place. I could not help worrying about Max. How will we find each other when he arrives in the city?

"What about all the other nuns?" I eventually asked Yuri, to break the silence.

"They have been sent to their home towns," he replied.

I thought about Alice, already on a train back to Nizhny Novgorod, I supposed. She and the others had risked their lives for me; I hoped they were safe.

~ *A Kind of Prayer* ~

Oh Max, my darling. Where are you now? Can you hear me?

It is seven days since we were separated at Nizhny, when you last held me and kissed me, and I watched you walk away between those two men. It seems longer. I miss you so much.

Every time I close my eyes, like now, I can see you ~ standing in the garden at Yekaterinburg, nervously introducing yourself, or sitting in your sister's kitchen, laughing with her as you told me about your childhood. And when all is quiet, like now, late at night, I hear your voice, singing to me that lilting song from Ukraine as you made love to me for the first time. Even my skin remembers your touch, and tingles again.

But now I am alone in a strange bed, and instead of escaping, my love, I am trapped here in Moscow, longing for you. The complex plan to get us to safety has floundered. The Abbess has been arrested, the convent is now closed, and I am in hospital for tonight. Thankfully, Sacha will make sure that I have somewhere to sleep until you arrive.

My mother has appeared, like an unwelcome ghost. She has become something in the Whites, telling everyone about my royal blood, so now they think I am their next queen; I dread to think what the Reds will do if they find out. If only it could have been Myriam who visited me, with her wise words, but I suppose her job is done now.

Take care, my love. I yearn for the moment when we are

together again.
Goodnight, darling.
I love you.

Chapter 3

~ *Moscow, Sunday 28 July 1918* ~

The doctors, satisfied that I was not suffering from anything worse than the surface wound to my forehead and the mild concussion the impact had caused to my brain, released me from the hospital the following morning, with instructions to rest. My head was tender, under the bandages, but the fierce ache of the previous day had subsided, at least partly, and I was declared fit to face the world. Clearly, since I was naked when I left the convent, I didn't have any of my own clothes, so the nurses gave me some (that had been donated, ironically, by the convent). Yuri had brought my nun's habit, but he had warned me not to wear it, as the new regime did not approve of religions, and some of the soldiers were ready to abuse anyone in monastic clothing. My only real possession, still around my neck, was the silver chain and birthstone pendant that had been given to me for my seventeenth birthday by Alexandra and Nicholas when we were in exile in Tobolsk together.

Sacha arrived in the ward to collect me; I was sitting in the chair beside the bed that was no longer 'mine'. She led me from the building and into the sunshine of another warm day. Then she confused me by opening the passenger door of a gleaming green motor car that was parked near the hospital doors. "Come on, jump in," she said, grinning at my amazed expression.

"This is yours? You can drive these things?"

"It's not so hard. I bought it to take my mother around, and the nice people at the garage showed me what to do."

I climbed carefully in, feeling the cold leather seat through my thin clothes and smelling the strange mixture of petrol, oil and paint that seemed to accompany every motorised vehicle. Sacha deftly swung the starting handle, then jumped in, slamming the door shut, making me wince as the vibration rattled my head. She manouvered us out of the hospital grounds, and soon we were winding through the city, the sickly fumes from the engine gradually building up and overpowering my delicate senses. Sacha chattered on, pointing out landmarks, oblivious to my growing nausea. In better circumstances, I would have enjoyed the experience, but in my tender state I was grateful when we stopped outside an apartment building and Sacha cut the engine.

* * *

Sacha and her mother lived on the third floor of what had once been quite a smart block of flats, though it was beginning to show signs of age and neglect. As we climbed the stairs together I felt a growing tension. Although I loved my friend, and was grateful that they were putting me up, I was dreading the expected inquisition when we were alone, about my motives and plans for the future. I resolved to avoid answering any questions.

However, it was nothing like that. I found that her mother was a very different woman from the one I had met at Alexander Palace, eighteen months earlier. The Countess Evgeniya Dolgorukov had aged visibly. Gone were the sharp eyes and insightful spirit; in their place was a woman who peered out at the world in fear and pain. She spoke little, and contributed nothing to the stilted exchanges between Sacha and me. The day passed slowly, and conversations with her were short.

"It is sad to see how she has declined," I commented to

Sacha in the evening, when her mother had retired to bed.

"She has been slowly fading away since the news of daddy's death. He was her whole world, and she lived every day in fear of what was sure to happen eventually. She hates the new order, and wanted you to accept your mother's plan. She was amazed when the news came that you had tried to sacrifice yourself."

I studied her face, to see if there was any sign of recrimination, but saw none. "You and Sofiya made a good case," I replied, "but I could not face the prospect of becoming a figure-head for more violence."

"I still think that you could be the best ruler for this country."

"But Sacha, that's just where I have the biggest problem. The people don't need a ruler, they need a leader, and they have chosen one."

"Lenin?" she prompted.

I nodded. "Yes, and whether you or I agree with their choice or not is unimportant. Even if it is the wrong choice, it is for them to make that decision and to live with the consequences."

"You agree with them, though, don't you?" She looked me in the eyes, probing.

"As a matter of fact, I do. Somehow, the idea of the people controlling their own lives seems right to me. I hate the fact that, up to now, the citizens have been handed down from one Tsar to the next like the crown jewels."

"But how much control can the people have?" she said, forcefully. "It seems to me that all they have done is replace a monarchy with a dictatorship. They are being ruled by a committee now, led by one man ~ what is so different?"

I was surprised at her summary, and unable to think of a response. "I admit it looks that way," was all I could manage, allowing the subject to drop.

"Anyway," she suddenly said, brightly, "it's getting late, I expect you are tired."

"Yes," I agreed, nodding tentatively. The dull pain pressing inside my temples had been building through the afternoon. I touched the bandage gently at the spot where the bullet had been deflected. Was it Myriam's doing? Had she saved my life by misdirecting the shot? "My headache has returned," I added, lamely.

She stood, and held out a hand to me. "Then you must rest. I'm afraid you are sleeping with me, we don't have a spare bed. When Sofiya stayed, I shared with my mother so Sofiya could have my bed ~ it was not satisfactory." She grinned. "You could sleep with her, if you prefer."

"Thank you, I think I like the first option better," I grinned, accepting the hand and rising slowly to my feet.

"Good! I've been wanting to share a bed with you since we first met," she said, then quickly turned away and headed towards the door, where she paused to wait for me, not meeting my eyes.

For a moment, I wasn't sure I had heard correctly, but her embarrassed reaction was clear; she meant what she had said. I reached her side, and squeezed her hand. "Come on then, lead the way," I said, smiling.

She took me to a small bedroom, pretty with floral covers and curtains, and a window that looked out over the glittering lights of the city. There she left me to undress and put on the nightgown that she had laid on the bed for me. When she returned, wearing her own nightie, I was between the covers.

She slipped in beside me, and we lay on our sides, looking at each other, holding hands. When I was younger, growing up as a servant at Alexander Palace, the twins and I had shared a room and a bed; we had slept together, like this, and sometimes not slept. Now I found comfort in the closeness of my friend.

Sacha read the tiredness in my eyes and smiled. "Goodnight," she said, softly.

"Goodnight, Sacha. Thank you."

We kissed, gently, then she turned her back to me, pressing her bottom into my tummy and hips. I snaked my hand between her waist and the arm that rested on it, and snuggled closer. I found a breast and, lightly stroking her skin, drifted into sleep.

Chapter 4

~ *Moscow, Monday 29 July 1918* ~

My first thought when I awoke the next morning was about Max. The travelling circus, in which he had been concealed from Avadeyev and his murdering cohorts, was due to pull into Moscow station on its own train sometime that day. At last the waiting would be over, and we would be together again.

With excitement building inside me, I opened my eyes. Beside me, Sacha was already awake, looking at me with a smile on her lips. We kissed lightly and held each other for a little while, stroking each other's skin with our fingers.

"I have to help mother in the kitchen," she said, eventually, slipping from my arms and out of the bed. I watched as she dressed, as slim and lithe as a deer. She left her wardrobe door open; "Take your pick from here," she said, waving a hand at the row of clothes hanging inside. "Most of my things should fit you."

I thanked her and, as she left the room, I climbed out of bed and looked through the clothes she had indicated, choosing a simple, long plain dress with patch pockets on the breast. While putting it on, I found that I was quietly singing again that Ukranian folk song, 'Oy u Hayu' ~ which translates as 'In A Forest Glade' ~ with which Max had serenaded me on the night we first made love.

* * *

After making the bed, I joined Sacha and Evgeniya in the kitchen for breakfast, a simple meal of bread and a boiled egg each.

"Do you have any idea where the circus will set up?" I asked as we ate.

Sacha shrugged, and looked to her mother to answer. "The only place I ever saw one was in Sokolniki Park," the older woman replied.

"Is that far from here?" I enquired.

"It's north of the river, you could probably get a tram," suggested Sacha.

"Aren't there usually posters announcing things like this, telling people where to go?" I looked from Sacha to her mother.

The old lady seemed unsure. "I haven't seen any, have you, Sacha?"

My friend shook her head.

It was a weird, disjointed conversation.

"I don't know what time their train will arrive," I added despondently, "or even which station."

Sacha reached out a hand to touch mine in a gesture of sympathy. I placed my own hand over it, and managed a wan smile, but I was distracted by a strange look on her mother's face, a twisting of the mouth, a lowering of the eyes. It was not something I could give a name to, or comment on, but it was odd. She would not meet my eyes, but picked at the remains of her meal on the plate before her. I registered it, recorded it as perhaps being significant, before turning back to my friend and smiling my thanks.

When we had cleared away the breakfast things, Evgeniya retired again to her room, and I sat still while Sacha removed the hospital dressing from my head wound. I saw her grinning as she unwound the bandage, and demanded to know what was so funny. She went to the bedroom and brought back a hand mirror which she held it out to me. When I looked into it, the first time I had seen myself for days, I saw that the hospital had completely shaved my head; all that remained of my lovely dark hair was a kind of blue shadow.

"I look like a Buddhist monk!" I spluttered. "They didn't have to shave it all off!"

"It would have looked worse if they left half behind, silly," she said, smiling broadly. "Then you would have looked like a clown!"

By that time, though, she was examining my wound. "You are really lucky to be alive," she admonished. "Another inch, and the bullet would have smashed right through your skull. It might even have gone into your brain, if it could find it."

Ignoring her dig, I studied the wound via its reflection in the mirror. It was a groove, about four inches long in total, running diagonally from a point near my hairline, above my right eye, ending above my right ear. The doctors had pulled the flesh neatly together with a line of stitches, and it was no longer bleeding, although Sacha showed me the yellow/brown stain on the dressing she had removed.

After she had applied a clean pad, and fixed it in place with a shortened bandage, we set about plundering her hat drawer for something I could wear to cover my bald head, eventually settling on a modern knitted bonnet with flaps that fell over my ears. It was the wrong time of year for it, really, but it was better than the bandage-and-shaved-head look.

* * *

"Would you like me to come with you to look for the circus?" Sacha asked as we washed the breakfast things.

I hesitated to impose on her further, but my need to find Max rose above every other thought. and she knew her way around the huge city. "Thank you," I replied,

29

gratefully. "I must try to catch him before he leaves the circus; if he goes to the convent to find me he could run into trouble, and he will have no idea what has happened to me."

She dried her hands and picked up the dishes, opening a cupboard door and putting them away. "I could give you a guided tour of the city in the process. We can leave the car at home and take the tram."

I grinned. "Perfect!"

Half an hour later we were sitting in an electric tram, clattering our way towards the city centre. It was a bright morning, and Sacha occasionally pointed through the window at some places of interest, but I was distracted, trying to spot any posters for the circus, without success.

The tram system in Moscow was a wonderfully complex, almost anarchic, spider's web of tracks that radiated from the city centre. By the time we rode it in 1918 it was almost all electrically powered, though there were still a few four- or six-horse trams run by eccentric old private operators. We arrived at the South Terminus, and switched to another line heading over the river and northwards. It was a double-decker, open at the top, giving a wonderful view as we crossed the Moskva on one of the beautiful stone bridges. The gantry above our heads hummed and fizzed on the power rail and the wheels clattered as the track intersected with others, sometimes causing a lurch as the vehicle changed direction. We looked down over the side ~ at the roofs of motor cars, the tossing heads of horses, and the hats of pedestrians enjoying a stroll in the sunshine ~ then up and beyond to the river, stretching silvery into the distance to our left and right. The wind blew in our faces, lifting my spirits. It was a lovely day to be out.

Sacha told me when to alight, and we hopped off

outside the new Saratovsky Railway Station, which received trains from the east and south.

Ignoring the passenger entrances, we skirted to a road at the side of the buildings to find the goods yard. Once through the gate, we scanned the jungle of tracks, looking for animal cages or painted wagons, but saw nothing that looked circus-like.

Some men were working beside a trainload of coal, and I nervously asked them if they knew anything about a circus train due to arrive; they shook their heads. One of them pointed out the yard manager's office, a shack behind the passenger building, on one of the platforms opposite. I thanked him, and we picked our way over iron rails and sleepers, and around long chains of stationery freight trucks, to the brick-built annex tacked onto the back of the main structure.

Inside, a secretary sat at a typewriter. She looked up in surprise when we entered. "Passengers are not allowed in the goods yard," she said sourly at once, glowering at us.

"We are not passengers," I explained. "We are here for information about a goods train that is expected today, carrying the circus."

"Circus?" she laughed. "There's no circus due here today, or any other day according to my schedule." She pointed to a chart on the wall, as though that made everything clear.

I was shocked, and found myself suddenly fighting back tears; I did not know what to do next. Sacha spoke for me. "What about Kursky station?" she suggested to the woman. "All the trains used to go there before Saratovsky was opened, would you know if ...?"

Already the woman was shaking her head. "You would have to ask them," she said, dismissively.

Sacha, bless her, was tenacious on my behalf. She

pointed to the woman's telephone. "Will you call them, please, and ask?"

With a sigh and pursed lips, the woman picked up the handset. She spoke to the operator, then waited, moving papers around on her desk. When she was connected to the other station, she said, curtly: "I have two women here asking about a circus train; are you expecting one?" After a pause, she nodded. "I thought so."

Hanging the little earpiece back on its cradle she turned back to us. "Nothing is expected there, either," she said, bluntly, ending the conversation by returning to her typewriter, hammering the keys loudly to indicate her displeasure at being disturbed, and to prevent any further conversation. It was clear that there was nothing to be gained by staying, so Sacha thanked her, with only a hint of sarcasm, though her gesture was ignored, and led me out onto the platform again.

We found a door to the passenger ticket area, and made our way through the crowds to the front, where we paused in the bright sunlight to collect our thoughts. My mind was in turmoil, I could not speak ~ it was as though the circus had never existed.

Back on the main street, we found a small café and sat for a while with a pot of tea to plan the next move.

I felt bereft, with no plan and no-one who could help. "Can we go to that place your mother mentioned?" I asked Sacha. "Perhaps they came early, or by road."

"Sokolniki Park? Certainly," she nodded, smiling reassuringly. "It's a pleasant ride from the city centre. Don't give up hope; I'm sure there is an explanation."

We finished our tea and caught a tram back towards the city centre, then hopped onto another heading for the western suburbs.

My heart began to pound with excitement when we

32

reached the park for, as we alighted from the tram, I could see the tops of colourful awnings among the trees, and crowds of people were filling the footpaths. I felt a smile filling my face, and I turned and hugged Sacha, who was also looking happy and relieved. I wanted to push past the families and couples who were moving too slowly for my liking, and run excitedly to the centre of the park, but managed to walk at a steady pace, craning my head to look past the crowd. I could hear music and smell hot food.

At last we reached the focus of all the activity, and I finally broke into a run as we entered the perimeter, leaving Sacha behind. But the smile fell from my lips and I stopped dead as I saw what we had found. It was a market, with stalls selling produce and crafts, and a small fair, with rides for the children. Tears suddenly erupted from my eyes and poured down my cheeks as I looked around in despair. There was no circus; my last hope had been dashed.

Chapter 5

~ *Aleksandra* ~

Sacha led me away from the pushing crowd to a quiet spot by a lake, and we stopped at one of the benches arranged along the side of the path. She put her arms around me and I sobbed into her shoulder.

We stood like that, and Sacha held me close, until my tears had ebbed and my breathing settled to something resembling normal, then she gently lowered me onto the bench and sat beside me.

As I regained control of my body, I felt my despair turning into anger. "I trusted too many people," I said, vehemently. "Someone has lied to me, and I need to get some answers."

Sacha looked puzzled. "Who? How?"

"I don't know for sure, yet, but I have my suspicions." I hesitated, then plunged on. "Your mother knows more than she is telling, Sacha. Did you notice how she responded this morning when I was asking about the circus?"

"She's not herself, Nata. Her world fell apart when daddy was killed. Half the time I think she is slowly shutting down, waiting to join him."

"I know, but I'm convinced that some of it is an act. She and Sofiya have been hiding something from me, I am sure."

"Your mother?" Now she was really surprised. "Why do you say that?"

"When she came to see me in the convent last week, with all her grand plans to make me Tsarina, do you remember that I insisted that she had to get Max and me to

England?"

"Yes, and I noticed that she seemed thrown by it."

I nodded, grimly. "Exactly. She knew that he would not arrive here. When she agreed, she was just humouring me to persuade me to agree to go along with her idea."

Sacha became thoughtful. "I will get the truth out of my mother," she said, suddenly, surprising me with the force of her reaction and jumping to her feet. "In fact, I am going home to tackle her right now!"

"Thank you," I responded, "but be gentle with her; she has suffered a lot. Perhaps Sofiya put pressure on her."

"Yes, but if you are right, then she has been deceiving me, too. What do you want to do next?"

"There is only one thing left that I can do, right now," I said, "and that is to return to the convent and wait for Max. If he comes, that is where he will be expecting to find me."

* * *

Once again we made our way back to the city centre and the busy terminus, where Sacha helped me to catch the right tram. "I will come to pick you up from the convent in my motor car at dusk," she promised, hugging me before I climbed onto the platform. I found an empty wooden seat and waved to her as, with a whining of electric motors and the now-familiar smell of hot grease from the wheels and sparks occasionally erupting as it collected its power from the cable stretched above my head, the tram set off.

It was not a long journey, ten minutes or so, and when the convent came into view, I nodded to the conductress, who rang the bell to stop the bus. I had seen some people hopping on and off while the vehicle was still moving, but I did not feel brave enough to try that.

When it came to a halt, I stepped down onto the pavement and looked across the square to where the two bell-towers, with their golden domes, rose above the church that formed the front of the convent. This was where I had sought sanctuary when I arrived in Moscow, where the nuns had made me welcome, and where my mother had suddenly re-entered my life, trying to persuade me to become the next Tsarina.

Two days ago, I had peered down from the top of that left-hand tower, my mind in turmoil, and watched as the soldiers took up their positions around this square. I was sure they had come for me, and, tired of running, I had surrendered to fate.

It was a strange feeling, now, standing where those men had been when I emerged from the dark, heavy doors. But, as the tram droned and clattered away, I saw that the church was the scene of some activity. The doors were open, and a cart was drawn up at the foot of the steps. People were carrying things up and into the building.

Curious, I crossed the road and approached. An assortment of chairs and tables remained piled on the cart, along with rolls of carpet and boxes of various sizes filled with everything from books to kitchen utensils. As I stood, uncertain what to do next, a woman emerged from the church doors and wearily descended the steps. She looked at me, blankly, and I smiled nervously.

"May I ask what is happening?" I said, then felt the need to explain: "I was a nun here until recently."

She returned my smile with her own, tired, version. "We are making a women's refuge," she replied, gesturing with a hand. "The sleeping quarters will be turned into a dormitory for homeless families, and the church is to become a soup kitchen."

Somehow, it struck me as a worthy use for the building. "Would you like some help?" I offered.

She studied my skinny frame, which admittedly was not

ideally constructed for hard work, but she did not comment on it. "I cannot pay you, but I would certainly be pleased to have another pair of hands," she said.

Her pretty oval face was etched with tiredness, her eyes had dark circles, and her wild hair was lank with sweat. She seemed to be ready to drop with exhaustion, and my heart went out to her. "I'll be glad to help in any way I can," I said sincerely.

At that moment a man came down the steps, grabbed some furniture and, with a glare at my companion and I, carried them inside. She ignored him and began to explain to me what was to be done with the things on the cart. Then another woman emerged from the building and descended to stand beside us, her head lowered in weariness. The first woman turned and took her arm. "This is my friend and assistant, Anna Itkina," she said by way of introduction. The woman raised her head and nodded.

"Hello Anna," I smiled. "I'm sister ... I'm Ephraimia. Call me Mia."

She returned my smile, and we shook hands.

"And I'm Aleksandra Kollontai," the first woman said. "Now, let's get on; we have much to do."

* * *

I grabbed a box of crockery and followed the other two into the church, adding my box to a stack that was growing against the wall just inside the inner doors.

The last time I had been there, I had looked around the nave at a colourful picture gallery of the saints, ranged beside and above each other on all sides like a permanent congregation of silent worshippers. Now the walls were bare, the grey stone dotted with lighter patches where the icons had been. The brightly painted screen at the far end was also gone, revealing the altar and leaving a large, clear room. The echoes remained, however. the clicks and scrapes as we moved and spoke, reverberating from the hard walls and far ceiling.

We laboured until the cart was empty and the sullen driver had taken it away, then we began laying out the tables and chairs. The rugs and books for the classroom we carried through the side doors into the ringing room and stacked them there temporarily. The bell ropes still hung mutely from the ceiling and the stone steps spiralled upwards ~ the steps on which I had sat and decided to die. What a strange turn of events it was that had brought me back.

At lunchtime, Anna heated some soup and we paused briefly to eat it with small pieces of bread, gazing around the room, discussing what to do next. The wide, carved, stone altar stood like a mute accusation of blasphemy, stripped now of its embroidered velvet drape and its gold candlesticks and chalices. I was told that the sacred sanctuary, where the the priests would conduct their secret rites (obscured from the view of the unworthy worshippers by the ornately painted screen) was to become a kitchen, and the altar would serve as the counter over which food would be dispensed to the needy of Moscow. I liked that ~ hot meals for the homeless and hungry seemed to me to be a more worthwhile use for it.

Another cart arrived and was unloaded. By late afternoon, we had created a reasonable eating hall in the nave, with seating for up to a hundred people at a time. We had also started to set up a classroom in what had previously been the nuns' chapel.

I noticed that Aleksandra began looking frequently at her watch, and eventually she announced that she and Anna had to leave, to attend a meeting. I volunteered to continue helping the next day, and she accepted gratefully, offering to pick me up in her motor car on her way in the morning. I gave her Sacha's address.

We parted at the steps, and I watched the two women walk off across the square and out of sight, then I sat on the steps to wait for Sacha. I realised that my head was throbbing; funny that I had not noticed it until then.

Oh Max my darling, where are you?

Tonight we should have been together, but the world is conspiring to keep us apart.

I will wait here for you, where we arranged to meet, every day until you return to me.

Chapter 6

~ *All Lies* ~

Sacha was subdued as she drove me back to her apartment in the fading light, the car's headlamps casting a smudge of yellow light on the road before us. She asked about my visit to the convent, and appeared to be listening as I told her about the changes happening there and the people I had worked with, but I could see that she was only half-concentrating. I guessed that the confrontation with her mother had been a difficult experience, and longed to know the outcome, but I could not ask about it. She would tell me at her chosen time.

Evgeniya was not to be seen when we entered the apartment, and the door to her bedroom was closed. Sacha made us a pot of tea and a salad for dinner. There was no meat ~ most foods were still in short supply, and all our meals were simple. She took a plate through to her mother's room, then returned to join me at the table. We ate in tense silence.

At last, as we stood to clear the table, Sacha paused, the crockery in her hands, and turned to face me. I felt a moment of dreadful foresight. "There is no easy way to tell you this," she said, softly. "I'm sorry Nata, the circus seems to have vanished."

It was not what I had been expecting. I felt as though the world had suddenly detached itself from me, and I was observing myself, standing alone in an echoing gallery. I stared at her, struggling to come to terms with the meaning of her words. If the circus was not coming, then where was Max? And why was it not coming? My day had begun in

41

excited expectation of his return, and now I found my head swimming at the disappointing news. An answer was clearly expected, but my mind could not make one. Sacha's voice reverberated in the void that suddenly filled my head; my legs became weak and tears began to flow from my eyes. I sat down again heavily.

Seeing my face fall, she put the plates back on the table and grabbed my hands. "It does exist, though," she continued quickly. "Mother says it's called the Revskovsky Circus. It forms up each year in the south at the beginning of summer, travelling northwards on barges, by canal and river to the Urals. Then it turns west, using its own train, along the Trans-Russia Railway calling at the main towns on the way to Moscow. From there, it works its way south again, and disperses in the autumn."

"Why didn't it come to Moscow?" I managed to ask.

"That's a mystery at the moment. It's not been seen since Kotelnich, the first stop after Nizhny, six days ago. And another odd thing is that the train it uses has been abandoned in a siding; they must have struck out by road, but no-one knows why, nor which direction they took."

"Strange behaviour," I commented.

She nodded, pensively, hesitating. I sensed another bombshell.

"That's not all," she said, hoarsely, looking at her feet.

Could it get worse? "Max?" I managed to ask.

She shook her head. "No. Oh, no. Something else," she whispered, "something ... unexpected."

I waited, puzzled.

With a deep breath, she raised her face until her eyes locked with mine. "Sofiya," she began, then hesitated.

"My mother?" I asked.

She nodded her head once, then changed the motion to a slow shaking, her lips tightening. "She's not your mother," she said.

"The woman who came with you to the convent is not my mother?" I repeated, slowly.

"That's right; I got it out of my mother this afternoon. She let something slip, while explaining about the circus, and I realised that there was more than she was telling me. I demanded to know what was going on, but she wouldn't say at first. I was so angry that I threatened to leave her here alone if she didn't tell me everything. She held out for a while, convinced I was bluffing, but when I started to pack a suitcase she admitted everything.

"It seems that I was pathetically easy to fool. I had never met your mother before, so when my mother told me that the woman who came here was her, of course I believed her. But the truth is that no-one knows where the real Sofiya is. That woman and my mother concocted this story between them to get you to agree to stand as Tsarina. I don't even know what her real name is ~ Mother wouldn't tell me, I think she's too scared ~ but it's not Sofiya Tereshchenko."

I should have been angry at the deception, but instead I felt a strange surge of relief. Three days earlier, when I met her for the first time, I could not understand why there was no bond between us; why, if anything, I had felt a barrier. This explained it. I smiled at my friend, and grabbed her in a hug.

"I was so worried that you would think I was in on the lies," she said as we resumed clearing the table. "After all, I kept trying to persuade you to go along with her plan."

"The idea never entered my head," I assured her. I followed her into the kitchen, and we began to wash the plates. "To be honest, I'm glad to be able to cross one name off my list of problems. I can wipe Sofiya from my mind, and concentrate on my priority ~ finding Max."

43

* * *

Over the following few days, the little team of Aleksandra, Anna and I finished preparing the centre, put up a sign over the front doors, and began to welcome our first guests. At first, there were few customers, but as the days passed and word spread, more and yet more arrived. By day three we were rushed off our feet from dawn to dusk, and I helped with anything I could, hoping it would take my mind off my growing depression over Max's non-appearance. It didn't.

Instead, every time someone entered through those big oak doors, my eyes were drawn to them, my mind assessing at once, from a distance, if they were tall enough to be him, or wide enough, or blonde enough.

Also on day three, Aleksandra held her first class for the children, in the room that had once been the nuns' chapel.

"Is all this charity work part of your job?" I asked at the end of the day, when we were in the car taking me home.

She laughed. "No, it's my hobby. The rest of my time is taken up with Party work, travelling up and down the country, talking to women's groups."

She seemed to be more important than I had realised. "What is your job?" I asked, all innocence.

"I run the Women's Commissariat, part of the government," she replied, looking at me oddly. "Did you not know?"

I was embarrassed at my ignorance. "No, I'm sorry. I have been rather out of things for a while."

"Oh, I'm not put out, I didn't mean to sound critical. It's nice that someone just wants to be part of what I'm doing without knowing who I am."

"I'm enjoying it," I said sincerely. "The truth is that I have time on my hands and I need a job."

As the driver stopped the car outside Sacha's apartment, she seemed to be deep in thought for a moment, before saying: "You can always work with me, I'm glad to have you on the team, but my department has no money, I cannot pay you any wages. However, one of my colleagues in another department needs a secretary; I could introduce you, if you like."

I smiled. "That would be wonderful, thank you. And I would still like to help you whenever I can."

She looked me in the eye. "Gladly, there is still much work to be done, not just in the soup kitchen, but in other areas of need, too. You could find that some of it will break your heart."

I nodded. "I'm beginning to see that, but my heart tells me that I must try."

"See you tomorrow, then," she grinned as I clambered out.

Chapter 7

~ *Thursday 1 August 1918* ~

A man entered the dining hall and stood looking around the room. As always, tuned to every arrival, I checked ~ it wasn't Max. For a while he didn't move, blocking the doorway as he took in the scene.

The place was busy, in the way to which we had become accustomed; we had few quiet spells. People pushed impatiently past him as they arrived or departed, chairs scraped, crockery clattered, voices droned, some raised in anger or laughter.

I could not help noticing him; he stood out from the crowd, for some reason I could not immediately resolve. It wasn't his build ~ he was as thin as any of them ~ nor was he any taller. He appeared to be about ten years older than me, with a neat little moustache, a beard that looked like a small letter 'w' stuck to his chin, and round spectacles on his nose. His hair was black, thick and curly. His clothes were of good quality, and clean, whereas those of most of the diners had seen better times. They consisted of a military-style jacket ~ high-collared, made of coarse wool, brown, with large, patch pockets. Ex-military wear was not unusual in the dining hall, many of our patrons had been soldiers who, returning home, had found that there were no jobs for them, but his clothes looked new.

Perhaps it was his eyes, bright and alert, or his confident demeanour ~ unlike the rest of our guests, he did not have the air of a man who had lost everything.

Eventually, he made his way between the tables and approached the counter that we had built over and around the altar, where I was serving. He picked up a tin tray and placed it in front of me, watching as I ladled some stew into a bowl and set it on his tray, adding a piece of bread and a spoon. Instead of moving on immediately, however, he caught my eye, then smiled. I was taken by surprise and quickly looked down, but smiled shyly in return. Then he was gone, weaving around the tables with his tray until he found an empty seat.

Anna was nearby, stacking clean dishes. She made a kissing sound with her lips to attract my attention, then grinned at me with raised eyebrows. I stuck out my tongue and turned to serve the next customer.

When the queue diminished, I relinquished my place at the counter to Anna, and began circulating the tables, picking up abandoned trays and bowls and wiping the surfaces clean. I reached the table where the stranger was sitting, and he caught my eye as he pushed his tray across to me, then indicated with a wave of his hand the empty chair opposite him. "Will you stay for a minute?" His voice was mellow, with a trace of an accent ~ American, perhaps?

I put my stack of trays and crockery on the table and sat without speaking, unsure of his motive.

He leaned towards me to speak quietly, as though he did not wish other diners nearby to overhear. "My name is Yakov Sverdlov; Aleksandra has told me that you are looking for a job."

'Ah,' I thought, *'that explains it.'*

I nodded. "I need to earn a wage. Are you able to offer me something?"

"Perhaps," he said with a slight twist of his head, a cross between a nod and a shake, "but I do not wish to discuss it here. Can you get away for an hour or two?"

I looked at the big clock on the wall above the kitchen.

Two-thirty. The main rush of diners had passed, though there would be a steady stream all afternoon ~ Anna could manage, and Sacha would not be picking me up until later. "I will have to check with Aleksandra,' I said, "but I'm sure she will allow it. Will you wait while I go to see her? '

He nodded, and leaned back in his chair, his hands behind his head. I picked up the trays and headed back to the kitchen to tell Anna what was happening, eliciting another smirk, then out of the door and along the corridor to the classroom. There, I quickly explained to Aleksandra, who smiled and gave her consent; she seemed to be expecting it.

* * *

As I emerged from the dining hall into the daylight beside Sverdlov, we found that a heavy shower had begun to fall ~ one of those errant clouds that appears unexpectedly from an otherwise unblemished summer sky, sprays warm water over the unprepared, then passes quickly over, moving on to bless a few more souls, before finally running out of ammunition and disappearing over the hills as though it had never existed.

We stopped in the doorway, and Sverdlov waved to a man, smart in army uniform, who was smoking a cigarette under the awning of a shop across the square. The man quickly dropped the cigarette and ran to an automobile parked nearby. He started the engine and drove to the church steps, then jumped out again and opened the passenger door for us to climb in.

Soon we were crossing the city. At first, we talked about the weather and the scenery, and Sverdlov asked if I knew Moscow well. I told him my cover story, that I had arrived only a few days earlier, on a pilgrimage from the small community of nuns at Nizhny Novgorod to the famous

Marfo-Mariinsky convent.

He nodded. "Which is now the soup kitchen and refuge. And that has made you homeless and jobless."

It was my turn to nod. "A friend has taken me in, but I do not want to impose on her kindness any longer than I can help."

"Of course," he said. "The job I can offer you is secretarial, office work; do you know what that entails, and can you do it?"

"Oh yes," I answered quickly. "I used to ..." I stopped suddenly, realising that I was about to say that I used to be secretary to the Duchess Tatiana ~ a slip that could have signed my death warrant. "I used to help the abbess with her office work," I said, instead. "I am literate and numerate, and can use a typewriter and keep accounts." I smiled, trying to appear proud of my achievements instead of flustered at my potentially fatal near-mistake.

He seemed to be satisfied. "You seem like an ideal candidate. When we reach the Kremlin, I will have to induct you into the Party before I can formally offer you the job, would you be happy with that?"

"The Kremlin? The Party?"

My confusion must have been obvious, because he looked at me with an amused expression. "You do not know who I am?"

Embarrassed, I shook my head. It was beginning to dawn on me that I was mixing with some rather influential people.

He laughed, and in words not very different from those spoken to me by Aleksandra two days previously, continued: "Do not worry. In fact, it is reassuring. I am not well known, and that suits me. I am Secretary to the Council of People's Commissars."

"I thought that was Lenin," I replied, trying to show that

I at least made an effort to stay aware of events.

He seemed unimpressed. "He is Chairman of the council, and leader of the Party; I act on his instructions and report back to him. You could say that Comrade Lenin deals with matters of state, while I am responsible for housekeeping ~ day-to-day matters."

"So my job will be secretary to the Secretary," I grinned. He looked quizzical, and I made a mental note to try to curb my unconventional sense of humour.

* * *

We drove along beside the river Moskva for a while, the car tyres making a hissing sound on the damp surface, and I enjoyed the view of the busy waterway. Then we swung north onto one of the elegant bridges that spanned the river, heading towards the Kremlin, sprawling like a sleeping dragon over acres of land, nestled into a curve of the river, a complex of churches, residences, state rooms, shops and offices.

The Kremlin was originally another royal palace, built and added to by generations of Tsars at enormous expense to the Russian people. I knew of it, but had never been there in all my time with the royal family. The name means 'fortress', and the palace was nothing less than a statement, a declaration of the power of the Romanovs over the citizens.

A red-and-white barrier blocked the entrance, guarded by soldiers. We stopped, and words passed between our driver and one of the men, who peered into the car through the open window. I heard Sverdlov's name mentioned, then mine. Apparently satisfied, the guard stepped back and the barrier lifted.

Once through, we drove around the perimeter of Red Square, a great open area at the centre of the complex, flanked by grand buildings, and really more of an unequal trapezium than a square.

"This is the garrison," Sverdlov informed me as the car cruised slowly past a great slab of a building that dominated one side, "and the Party headquarters. This is where we will enrol you, and where you will work. My office is up there." He pointed towards the rows of windows in the walls above our car.

I found myself laughing, and shaking my head. I had spent my childhood encased in luxury, hating the disparity between my life and those of the poorer citizens, but now that the royal family was gone the people's representatives replacing it were getting a taste for the good life. "I never imagined that the new order would slip so easily into the shoes of the old," I said, choosing my words carefully.

He grinned. "Why not? It is rather symbolic, do you not agree?"

"But you must see the irony of it. All this was stolen from the poor." I waved my hand in a circle to indicate the ostentation all around us.

"Ah," he responded, wagging a finger. "The difference is that it belongs to all the people now."

* * *

The car came to a stop at the entrance to the garrison, and Sverdlov opened his door and hopped out, holding it for me. The sun had re-appeared, peeping from the edge of the shower cloud, creating a rainbow that seemed to rise symbolically from the horizon.

I slid from my seat and out into the warm afternoon air; wisps of steam rose from the pavement all around in the sunlight that twinkled on droplets hanging like jewels from window-sills and rooftops. I turned to stare across the wide expanse of the square, with Saint Basil's Cathedral away to my left at one end ~ almost ethereal with its beautiful, golden towers ~ and the stunning red-brick structure of the National Historical Museum, looking for all the world like an iced cake, closer, at the other end, on my right. Opposite, the domes of another church reared from a ragged row of rooftops.

There were sentry boxes beside the entrance to the garrison, and at intervals along the walls, and smartly-uniformed guards were marching slowly between them with that exaggerated step of theirs, stopping when they met, slapping their rifles and turning in a slow-motion pantomime of stamping feet, to march back again.

A shiver ran through me as I realised that I could finally be coming close to actually taking part in the future of Russia, more than at any other time in my life, despite my privileged upbringing.

"What is your opinion? Do you want to be part of this?" my companion asked from close beside me, a hint of pride in his voice.

I started; for a second I had forgotten that he was there. I smiled and nodded.

"Good. Let's go inside and get you signed up, then," he said, extending an open palm towards the entrance, like a Master of Ceremonies or a tour guide.

He led me up a couple of steps, through the tall, wide doors and along a corridor, turning eventually into a large hall. There he stayed with me while I filled in my application for Party membership, adding his signature to the form as my sponsor. Then, while I was taken to a room to have my photograph taken, he left to attend to some matters of his own.

Half an hour later, when he returned, I was still sitting on one of the rows of hard, wooden chairs, among a dozen or so other applicants, waiting for my membership card to be drafted. With a nod and a small smile, he took a seat beside me and we waited together.

Eventually my name was called and we walked to the little window, where a clerk passed the little red booklet into Sverdlov's outstretched hand. He opened it and flipped the pages, studying the contents, then grinned as he handed it to me. "Welcome to our club."

I looked at it for a moment, a small object with huge significance for me, a symbol that I had stepped from one side of a line to the other. A cover of red card with, inside, a page setting out my identity details ~ there was the photograph they had taken, and Sverdlov's signature to authorise my membership. I tucked it pensively into the pocket of my dress.

"I should be getting back to Aleksandra," I told him.

"Yes, of course; I will arrange a car for you. And I will pick you up from your friend's apartment at eight o'clock on Monday morning to start work."

I nodded, suddenly nervous. "Thank you for taking me on."

* * *

"You're going to work for whom?" Sacha screeched incredulously when I told her about my job on my arrival home. "Is this part of your suicide plan?"

I shrugged. "I needed to get a job," I mumbled, my excitement squashed.

"Why? I told you that you can stay with us for as long as you need to. You know I like having you here. Oh, Nata, this is not good. If they find out who you are, your desire to die will be quickly realised."

"I don't really want to die, Sacha, not any more. And, anyway, he's very nice," was all I could say.

She glared at me, her head tilted. "Nice? He's the

enemy, Nata." She pointed at the world beyond her window. "We are not the same as them. They want to kill us all. I know you sympathise with them, but you are still one of us." Her voice was rising in volume and pitch as her emotions swelled. "Look what they did to Nicholas and Alexandra, to their children ... to the servants for fuck sake!"

I was stunned as her anger escalated. I had never heard her swear, never seen her mouth so contorted. I turned away and went over to her settee to sit down, unsure what to say or do. After a moment, she dropped onto the cushion next to me, breathing heavily, and we sat in silence.

Eventually I took her hand. "Sacha darling, you are a wonderful friend, and I am grateful for all you have done for me. But I can't stay with you forever; your mother is finding it difficult to face me, and, to be honest, it is hard for me to resist telling her how angry I am at her deception, both to me and to you. Anyway, I must start supporting myself soon."

"I understand what you're saying, Nata, but you don't have to take such a dangerous job. Please wait for something safer to come along."

"There are not many jobs to be had, Sacha. The economy is in tatters. Besides, as long as I am careful, how can they possibly find out?"

Chapter 8

~ *Monday 5 August 1918* ~

After an uncomfortable weekend, in which Sacha's mother remained locked in her room, refusing to emerge while I was there, I was glad when Monday morning arrived and I prepared for my first day at work. Sverdlov collected me at eight o'clock as arranged, in an army car painted dull brown, green and black in apparently random splotches, with a red star on each door and a flag fluttering at the front. After a short drive, we pulled up at the garrison and he led me through busy corridors ~ where people, mostly men, mostly in uniform, were earnestly going about their business ~ and up two flights of stairs. Eventually, we stopped at a door.

"This will be your office," he explained, as he breezed in ahead of me.

It was a surprisingly large room, with the expected desk beneath large windows on the far side, and the walls lined with shelves and tall, grey filing cabinets. A crumpled, worn square of brown-and-green carpet failed to reach the extremities of the floor, leaving bare floorboards exposed around all its edges, while luxurious flocked wallpaper, dotted with grotesque shapes in lurid shades of green, crimson and gold, lurked behind the furniture.

Using an extended arm and Master of Ceremonies open hand he indicated a door in the wall to our left. "That door takes you to my office," he said. "And that one," indicating a similar one to the right, "is where Aleksandra works when she's here." He grinned, suggesting that she was most often not there. "You will be sharing your time between us. Although my department will be paying your wages, I won't be needing you all the time, and Aleksandra's department has no money, so this is my way of helping her out."

"What is actually required of me? What will I be doing?" I asked.

"Well, for me you will be opening the post and sorting it, filing, typing minutes and some of my letters, keeping my appointments diary and making sure I'm where I need to be at any time. Aleksandra will likely want you to do something similar, but she can use you as she likes."

I was about to ask another question, but he held up a hand to stop me, pulling a grand old pocket watch from his waistcoat and looking down at it like a character from Charles Dickens. "I have to leave you," he said, suddenly in a hurry. "There's a meeting of the Council; I must be there." He swept his arm in another expansive gesture. "Make yourself at home here, learn where everything is. This is your domain, now, so arrange things how you want them. I'll be back in a few hours."

With another grin and a wave, he disappeared through the door into his office in a swirl of dust.

* * *

I opened the top drawer of one of the filing cabinets and peered inside; it was empty. Puzzled, I checked the next, and the next, finding them all equally void. Amused, I moved to the cabinet beside it, which was also empty. The last one, however, held a shock ~ the top drawer was stuffed full with papers, but not organised, they had just been stuffed in, apparently at random. So much for Sverdlov's filing system.

Happy to have something to occupy my mind, I cleared a space on my desk ... my desk! ... and began to remove things from the filing cabinet. I read the heading of each item, and started to discern a pattern ~ correspondence, some bills, speeches, pamphlets ~ making a stack for each obvious category, and one for those of which I was unsure.

When Sverdlov returned, a couple of hours later, I was happily sorting through a sea of papers. "Ah," he said, rather embarrassed. "Sorry it's such a mess. There never seems to be time ..." His voice trailed off into a mumble.

I smiled. "Don't worry, it's what I'm here for."

Sheepishly, he retreated into his own lair, and I carried on working. At some stage, he reappeared with a cup of tea and a sandwich. He was so considerate, I had to hide a smile, but I also realised that tea-making was probably another of my jobs. I made a mental note to find out where the facilities were kept.

Mid-afternoon, he popped his head through the door. One filing cabinet had been labelled and filled with sorted papers, and I was starting on the second drawer-full of confetti. "Do you feel like stopping for a break?" he asked. "I have an hour free, and I'm going to the park; you can come, if you like."

I looked at the fresh heap on my desk, then at the bright afternoon sun streaming in through the window, making beams in the floating dust. It was not a hard decision I grinned. "Da!"

* * *

Our driver for this trip, a small man in army uniform, drove us along a broad road beside the river, then swung the car through wrought-iron gates into a park, where he stopped by a café. Sverdlov climbed from the vehicle and held the door open for me. Couples and small groups of people were walking in the afternoon sunshine, some of the women carrying parasols, some men wearing the colourful national costume of tunic and loose trousers. The trees were scarcely swaying in the slightest of breezes. Outside the café, tables and chairs had been set out on the grass, and couples sat with glasses of wine or cups of tea or coffee.

As we set out to walk together across a lawn dotted with beds of flowers and sprinkled with daisies, I found myself suddenly uncertain and reluctant to begin conversation. Though he was treating me with respect and kindness, and he seemed to be relaxed, I could not forget that he was a high-ranking official in the new government; not only my employer, but also part of the system that hated everything I had grown up accepting as normal.

So we walked in silence until we joined a path that wove through the shrubs beside a glistening lake. Many trees were still in bloom, and there were neat borders beneath them. Here and there, gardeners were at work among masses of summer flowers. The perfume was heady and restful.

"You are thoughtful," he said, gently.

I nodded, thinking about every word before speaking. "My life has changed dramatically," I finally replied. That much at least was true, but I could not tell him more, nor could I risk him asking too many direct questions. "You have been very kind to me, but I don't know anything about you," I said, after careful thought, diverting the conversation away from me.

He smiled. "Well, I was born in Nizhny Novgorod, forty-three years ago. I have two sisters and five brothers, and I am unmarried." As he said the last word, he stopped and turned, meeting my eyes and holding them until I had to shyly look down. He was interested in me! How much more complicated could my life become?

He took my hand ~ it was a surprise, but not unpleasant

~ and we began to walk again. "And now you must tell me about yourself," he said, assertively. The moment I had been dreading had arrived.

"You know almost everything from my Party application," I said, dismissively, shrugging my shoulders, desperate to turn the conversation away from my life.

"Oh, I know your name, and that you were raised by the nuns in Nizhny. Isn't that a coincidence? We were living in the same city; so close, yet we never met. But why were you with the nuns? And what kind of things do you like to do? What makes you happy?"

I smiled, and swept my free hand in an arc, indicating the scenery. "Actually, this. I am always most at ease when close to nature. I like to watch birds, and to draw them."

We reached the far end of the lake, and I paused to take in the pleasant sight: the sun glistened on the ripples; ducks, geese, coot and swans were swimming in their little groups, or just resting on the warm mud at the water's edge. People, mostly in twos or threes or fours, strolled past.

He turned his head to gaze at me, thoughtfully, a small smile on his lips. "I come here whenever I can, to remind myself that there is more to life than speeches and meetings and arguments and wars."

It was the first time I had seen him truly relaxed; most of the time he seemed to be in a permanent state of tension. I had noticed the way he chewed his nails and picked at the skin around them until they sometimes bled. He was thin, his cheekbones stood out beneath eyes that seemed to vanish into black pits; his passion for his work consumed him. But here, in the park, with the sun warming his pale skin, I began to see something of the real Yakov Sverdlov.

"You work too hard," I told him.

He smiled wryly. "There are not enough of us willing to

take on the responsibility," he said, shrugging his shoulders. "I did not really want this job, but no-one else would step forward."

We returned to the winding path that followed, approximately, the perimeter of the lake. Flocks of sparrows, feeding in the dappled shade beneath the trees, scuttled off into the bushes as we passed, though they didn't fly away ~ I saw that they waited there until it was safe to emerge again. Yakov had not released my hand, and I felt that I was being unfaithful to Max, because I was enjoying the company and the closeness.

* * *

"I have heard that Lenin ordered the killing of the royal family," I said, reluctant to spoil the mood, but scared of where it was leading, and hoping to learn something that might lead me to Max.

His lips visibly tensed. "Revolution is not about cosy chats in coffee shops," he replied, suddenly defensive. "Nor is it all about marches and demonstrations. The royals were not prepared to give up their comforts or their power easily, and used methods against us that were every bit as brutal as anything we have committed. In the years since this began, I myself have been imprisoned and exiled, as have just about all my comrades. Many brave people have been murdered. You have to understand that the Tsar and his family were part of a world-wide financial empire that, between them, own most of the Earth's resources. They were never going to hand over their share of that without a fight."

I studied him, carefully. He was earnest and sincere; there was a fervency about him that was infectious. And he was so thin! He looked as though a gust of wind could carry him away.

"I'm sorry," I said. "I did not mean to sound critical."

He squeezed my hand. "There's no need for you to be sorry. You were not part of it. Your life was dedicated to doing what you thought was right."

How wrong he was! I had been at the heart of the conspiracy, though I did not understand it at the time, and would have been horrified if I had known what was really going on. With a little shiver, I sensed that my whole life had been leading to this. For all my royal blood and privileged upbringing, I was always a rebel, on the side of the ordinary citizen. With the deaths of the Tsar and his family, I was freed from my fealty to the monarchy, although I was unsure about my new role as a servant of the people.

And there was Max. How could I tell Sverdlov about him? I was supposed to be a nun, for God's sake!

I needed Max, but what had happened to him? I wished I could talk it over with him, have him beside me. I needed him, every part of me yearned for him, ached for him to be there. Because, perverse though it may have seemed, my job with Yakov was offering some kind of hope for the future ~ dangerous, perhaps, but a better future than we had dared hope for. If only I could find my beloved Max.

* * *

We returned to work, Sverdlov to his meeting, I to my mountain of filing. When the drawer was organised, I went through the door into his office. He was back from his meeting, sitting at his desk, scribbling on a sheet of paper, and I asked for his appointments diary.

With a surprised expression, but no comment other than a raised eyebrow, he looked up from his own paperwork and handed over a fat, leather-bound book. Back at my desk, I sat and opened it, not sure what I expected to find.

It was filled with scrawled notes that, at first, I found hard to read. After a while, though, I began to see a pattern in the hieroglyphics.

An hour later, at five o'clock, I peeped into his office. "I have to go," I told him. "My friend will be expecting me for dinner." I placed the diary on his desk. "And you have to address the shopkeepers soon."

He groped in his waistcoat pocket and pulled out his watch ~ making me think for a moment of the white rabbit in Alice In Wonderland ~ then pulled a face. "Damn, yes! I can't give you a lift home. But I will walk down to the car pool with you and get one of the drivers to take you."

I thanked him, and we made our way along the corridor and down the stairs. He led the way through the maze of passageways until eventually we emerged from the back of the building into a large courtyard. Along one side of the square were stable doors, where men worked, brushing down horses, cleaning out soiled straw and filling feed and water troughs, on the other side stood a row of cars, their drivers polishing the paintwork or poking at the engines. A row of small carriages, Phaetons, was also parked nearby, their horses stamping impatiently. A driver appeared from the nearest one and lowered the step for me to climb up.

"This is Miss Nestorova," Yakov informed him. "She works for me. Please inform your colleagues that she is to have access to a vehicle at any time."

The man nodded and touched his cap. I climbed in and gave him directions to Sacha's apartment, then settled into the hard leather seat, waving goodbye to Yakov. The driver flicked the reins, and the cab lurched forward with a clatter of horseshoes and metal-rimmed wheels on the cobblestones. The age of the motor car may have been dawning, but the horse would still rule for a while longer.

Chapter 9

~ *Wednesday 7 August 1918* ~

One of the first challenges of my new job was learning to use the modern Underwood No.3 typewriter, a heavy machine that took up a sizeable portion of my desk space. I had a little typing experience, but not much. There were typewriters at Alexander Palace ~ ancient, little, spidery devices ~ but we rarely used them, as Tatiana and her mother preferred to write their letters freehand. However, with the help of the little instruction booklet I soon mastered it, and after a few days I even began to enjoy using it.

With the filing organized, I found I had time on my hands, and began to pester both Yakov and Aleksandra for more work. They gave me the minutes of their meetings to type, and their speeches, and letters. I was also able to help Aleksandra occasionally with the refuge at the convent, and to visit with her another project, a school for orphans in one of the ghettos.

We took a motor car from the pool, and as we wound through the streets of Moscow, I gazed around with interest at the contrasting images of the city, much of which I had not seen before. At first, around the Kremlin, there were affluent shopping areas, with well-dressed people bustling in the warm, mid-day sunshine. But, a few turnings on, these began to be replaced by dilapidated tenements, with washing lines looping between them across the street, sullen groups of men smoking pipes, and ragged children pausing in their play to watch us pass. It was in such a road that we stopped, to my surprise, and disembarked. We stood in the shadows cast by the grey, sad buildings that loomed above us. Rubbish was piled in corners, paint flaked from broken doors and grimy windows; the area was weighed down with poverty. Without hesitation, though, Aleksandra headed towards the nearest door, and I followed, somewhat anxiously.

There, two men leaned menacingly against the wall, and pushed themselves upright at our approach. I turned nervously to Aleksandra, but she was unconcerned, and addressed each man by name. Their world-weary faces cracked with welcome as they answered. She then introduced me to them, explaining that I was helping her, and they each held out a grubby hand to greet me. I accepted with a relieved smile, resisting the urge to wipe my hand on my dress afterwards. Their guard duty done, they stepped aside and allowed us to enter the building.

Inside, the air was heavy with the smells of poverty ~ stale cooking, dust, tobacco smoke and, yes, urine. Yet, not far off, I could hear the sound of children laughing, and it was towards that sound that we began to walk.

* * *

In a large, bare room, we found a group of children waiting. They were dirty, dressed in rags, the poorest of the poor in a city that had known extremes of wealth and poverty. She called them into a circle around us, and we sat on the floor among them. "This is my friend, Mia," she announced to them.

"Hello, everyone," I said to the circle of upturned faces. "Now I must learn all your names."

The rest of the afternoon passed easily, as I got to know each of the waifs and helped them to say my name. I found my admiration growing for the amazing woman who cared so much about them and seemed to have so much love to give. She organized simple games for them, but I noticed that, as they played, she was building them up, encouraging them, educating them. It was wonderful to see the smiles on their faces and the growing confidence in the way they carried themselves.

Yakov had left for a week, travelling out of Russia on diplomatic errands to Finland and Germany, so I spent all my time with Aleksandra. There was something that drove her, a passion inside that kept her going long after her body was physically exhausted. I did not know where it came from, but I had to keep up with her as, over the next few days, we bounced from one task to another, in the office and around the city, scarcely pausing for breath.

Back at the Kremlin, we worked on plans and preparations for a trip she was to take, out of Moscow, to visit the 'textile' towns that ringed the city, stretching North to Petrograd and as far east as Orekhovo-Zuyevo. These towns represented the heart of the Russian textile industry, and were the birthplace of much of the support for the revolution. Aleksandra was contacting the various unions in the factories, the Party representatives of each district, mill managers, town leaders and council officials. There were also security arrangements to be made and train tickets to be bought, as well as informing her colleagues in the other departments of the People's Council of the progress of the arrangements.

The telegraph room was on the ground floor, and at least once every hour I trotted down the two flights of stairs to deliver new messages and collect replies. I saw the names Lenin, Stalin and Trotsky in the addresses and the text of the slips of paper I carried, and experienced a thrill when I also saw those same names on the doors of offices I passed in the corridors. This was the heart of the new Russia, where charismatic and ambitious men made decisions that were bringing about their vision of the future, and, with Aleksandra, I was part of it.

* * *

At the same time as all this organising, Aleksandra was also dealing with the regular daily business that went with her position at the head of the Women's Congress. This involved receiving delegations from various organisations, visits to factories in Moscow, public meetings, and, of course, the orphanages. She involved me in everything, and I was extremely grateful to her. To be taught by such a great woman was a rare privilege.

But she was also a human being, and, along with all this work, I discovered that she had matters of her personal life to reconcile, which brought a surprise.

Sverdlov arrived back and came to call on Aleksandra. He stood in the doorway of her office. "It's Pavlo," he said to her, but seemed reluctant to say any more in my presence

Sensing that it was a private matter, I suggested that I could check the telegraph room for new messages, but Aleksandra shook her head. "No," she said, acknowledging my gesture with a hint of a smile of gratitude, "you need to know. Doubtless it will crop up occasionally. Pavlo is my husband. He has a habit of getting into trouble. He is a very brave man, a soldier, but foolish and weak-willed when it comes to alcohol and women."

She nodded to Yakov.

Obviously feeling uncomfortable, he told her: "He has been arrested again, in Ukraine."

I saw her lips tighten. "You're not telling us everything, Yakov dear. Was he with a woman?"

He nodded. "Yes, I'm sorry. A prostitute."

She turned to me. "When I first met Pavlo, it was his

68

wildness and independence that attracted me. But it has become tiresome and an embarrassment. I see him only once or twice a year; sometimes he doesn't come home at all. I still love him as much as ever, but I wish we had not married."

Returning her attention to Sverdlov, she said, with a sigh: "Will a letter from me get him out?" Yakov nodded again, and she continued: "Very well. I will write something and Mia will type it."

He handed her an envelope he was holding. "This has the details of the charges and where he is being held. I have included a note with the name and address of the Commissioner of Police."

As he turned to leave, she added: "Thank you, Yakov, you are a good friend."

Chapter 10

~ Thursday 8 August 1918 ~

As well as the pressure of my new job, I also needed to find somewhere to live, a home of my own that would be convenient for work. With no money until my first pay-day, still two weeks away, I was forced to pawn my necklace ~ the one given to me by the royals for my seventeenth birthday, and my only possession of value, since everything else I owned had been left behind when I fled the bloodbath in Yekaterinberg.

Sacha accompanied me as I viewed a number of apartments, and I was grateful for her opinions. Eventually, I used most of the money to pay the deposit and a month's rent on a furnished studio flat, and, with the few Rubles that remained, I bought some sturdy, practical clothes for work, so I could return the garments that Sacha had lent me.

From the window of my new home, on the top floor of a block only ten minutes walk away, I could see across the rooftops to the towers of the Kremlin, golden and sparkling, almost close enough to touch, and beyond them the river, wriggling like an eel through the centre of the city.

It was a simple room, clean, with just a bed, a wardrobe and chest of drawers, a table with one chair, and a compact kitchen area in one corner; I shared a bathroom and toilet with the three other tenants on that landing. It was all I needed ~ somewhere to sleep, and to study. Each evening I would return to my little nest with my arms full of books and pamphlets, lent to me by Aleksandra, and I would read and make notes far into the night.

It was a constant source of amazement to me as I discovered how little I really knew. In my time at Alexander Palace, I had tried to keep up with the news, but as I read the literature that I brought home each evening from Aleksandra's collection, publications that had never appeared in the royal libraries, I began to discover things that amazed and shocked me.

"I had no idea they were so callous," I told her as I returned a leaflet about the Bloody Sunday massacre ~ when a crowd of about three thousand citizens had marched peacefully to the Winter Palace to ask the Tsar for help, and had been fired on by soldiers at the gates. "I mean, I read about 'incidents' like this, but it was always portrayed as a matter of law and order."

"I was there, in the crowd," she answered, grimly, "that's why I wrote that leaflet. Nicholas was not the gentle man he tried to portray. The palace was not under threat ~ father Gapon, an Orthodox priest who led the march, just wanted to hand over a message of loyalty to him. But the fact is that he was not even in Saint Petersburg at the time of the massacre, it was probably the Empress who ordered the soldiers to open fire. It was widely known that Alexandra had no time for the working classes, she regarded them as nothing more than animals, but to order the soldiers to attack them ... it sickens me to remember that day. I am ashamed to share the same name."

She put the leaflet back in its drawer, then turned to me as I sat at my desk. "There is much more like that, Mia, my friend; I suspect that you soon will hate them as much as I do."

* * *

I enjoyed my early morning walks to work. The late-summer air was warm and pleasant, even at that early hour, and my shadow, cast by the low sun behind me, pointed the way ahead to a new day, filled with exciting new experiences. I sauntered along the pavement, past a row of shops ~ grocers, butchers, greengrocers, each with its now-familiar queue ~ then crossed the road towards one of the pedestrian entrances in the high wall that surrounded the Kremlin.

As I walked along the pavement beside the wall, my attention was caught by a young man at the kerbside a short way ahead, trying to start his automobile. He crouched at the front of the car, shouting abuse at the reluctant engine, while vigorously turning the starting handle. Motor cars were becoming a more common sight by then, but his behaviour was amusing because of his obvious frustration. Eventually, the machine burst into life with a cloud of smoke from the exhaust, and he ran to the side and jumped in. So interested was I that, even when I reached the arched opening in the thick wall, by which I was to enter the Kremlin gardens through a heavy oak gate, I paused to see him drive off.

As the car lurched forwards, he appeared to lose control, and the vehicle veered onto the pavement, hurtling towards me, the engine roaring loudly. I tensed to jump aside, but there was a lamp-post set in the pavement ahead, and as he tried to negotiate the gap between it and the wall, he found that the car was just too wide and, with a horrible scraping noise, it came to a sudden halt, wedged in the space. I could not help laughing at his ineptitude. With more loud revvings, he managed to reverse the car, tearing pieces off it as he did so, then, to the sound of crashing gears, plunged forwards again into the road.

At this moment events suddenly became very frightening. As soon as he had passed the lamppost, instead of continuing along the road, he again swerved onto the pavement, heading directly at me. Realisation dawned on me that perhaps this was not just bad driving, but a deliberate attempt on my life.

I had a split second to act. I jumped into the archway for protection, and pressed my back against the gate, facing the road, groping behind me for the heavy iron latch. But there was no time to open it before the car slammed diagonally into one side of the arch, more bodywork flying off as it came abruptly to a halt with one wheel only an inch from my body. I could feel the heat of the engine, and see the driver's face through the shattered wind-shield, wild eyes glaring at me from beneath a cap, his face twisted in a grimace of hate.

More crunching of gears preceded another reversing, as I desperately fumbled with the clasp of the gate, then the wreck was hurtling towards me again. I felt the latch finally release in my hand, and the gate gave way behind me. I fell through on my back into the gardens beyond, just as the car again hit the stonework, this time penetrating far enough to have crushed me, had I still been trapped against the gate. Twisting onto my knees on the brick path, trying to regain my feet, I saw the man's hands suddenly appear before his face, holding a pistol, pointed at me. I leapt to one side, stumbling, falling and scrambling, seeking the protection of the wall, and heard shots and pinging sounds as the bullets ricocheted from the stone blocks of the arch and the path where I had first fallen.

I struggled to my feet, hampered by my long, heavy skirt, and began to run along beside the wall, trying to put distance between us. I heard the roar of his engine and more scraping of metal on stone as he again reversed out of the arch, and I realised that he could not pursue me on foot as the hulk of his vehicle was blocking the entrance. I had gained precious seconds.

Not daring to look over my shoulder, I ran until I reached a small, square building that stood among trees, close to the wall. There I met a small group of people coming out of the doors, drawn by the commotion nearby. Some were priests, and I saw that the building was a chapel, with an icon of Jesus above the door and a traditional, onion-shaped, domed roof. One of them, an elderly man, hurried up to me. "What is happening?" he asked, anxiously, looking at my dishevelled appearance.

Delayed shock was making me shiver, and he put his arms around me reassuringly. "A man in a car was trying to kill me," I blurted, pointing towards the gate. His two younger colleagues immediately swept past me, their robes flying, and ran to the opening.

"Don't be afraid," the old priest said soothingly, "You are safe now." He led me into the chapel, and sat me on a wooden bench just inside. Some women were gathered there, and one was despatched to bring hot tea. We talked, and I described what had happened.

The younger priests returned a few minutes later. "We spoke to some bystanders," one of them explained. "Your attempted assassin has fled the scene. Apparently, a few people tried to apprehend the man as he ran from the wreckage of the car, but were prevented by two armed men, who escorted him away."

"Who would do such a thing?" one of the women asked.

I shook my head. "I really have no idea," I replied. Secretly, though, I could not help but think it might have been one of Avadeyev's men, caught up with me. If so, I was in real danger, and could be exposed at work at any time.

I sipped my tea, self-control slowly returning. When it was finished, I stood. "Thank you all for your help," I said sincerely. "Now I really must get to work."

"This should be reported," said one of the younger men. The others nodded sagely.

"I will tell my employer," I assured him.

The two young priests walked with me to the garrison building and on up to my office, then left me in the care of Aleksandra.

When they had departed, I told Aleksandra everything that had happened. "I cannot think why anyone would want to kill me," I said again, aware that I was not being honest with her.

"We have many enemies," she stated simply as she examined my hands, scratched and puffy from my fall and scrambled escape. "I will arrange security guards for you; I am angry with myself for not thinking of it sooner."

"Security?" I said. "Why would you expect me to need security?"

"All of us in the commissariats have guards with us at all times," she answered, waving an arm to indicate everyone in the building. "The counter-revolutionaries would love to bump one of us off ~ just think of the propaganda they could generate. Lenin has a small army with him, wherever he goes."

"And you?" I asked. "I've never seen any bodyguards since I've known you."

She shrugged her shoulders, and raised an eyebrow. "Two men from the secret service accompany me whenever I go out. That you have not seen them is a tribute to their ability to remain inconspicuous."

"Yes, but that's you, and Lenin and Trotsky, you are prominent members. But no-one is interested in me," I said.

"On the contrary, Mia dear, somebody seems to have taken against you. I suppose you are a very desirable target, because you are close to Yakov and me." She picked up her telephone, lifting the earpiece from its cradle and holding the speaking trumpet close to her mouth.

"Department thirteen, please, Natasha," she said into it after a moment, then smiled at me as she waited to be connected. Another pause, then ... "Kollontai. Yes. Please be so good as to send two agents to my office for permanent assignment to Comrade Mia Nestorova, Comrade Sverdlov's secretary." I heard some scratchy sounds from her earpiece. "Yes," she replied, "that is correct," then hung up.

She then stood and crossed to a cupboard behind the door, and took out a first-aid box, which she carried to her desk. Then she brought the basin and ewer from the stand in the corner and began to bathe my hands with disinfectant, drying each carefully.

"Any other injuries?" she asked, and I hitched up my skirt to show her my grazed knees. I was surprised to find that they were bleeding quite badly. These, too, she cleaned, then wrapped a gauze bandage around each.

She was just replacing the first-aid box in its cabinet when a tall, muscular man in a tight-fitting, dark suit knocked and entered the office. He introduced himself as Vasily, and escorted me to my own room. There he explained to me about the security arrangements for protecting Party members, inside and outside the Kremlin, and asked for details of my routines, where I lived, and so on. He also asked me to tell him everything about the morning's incident. It was all very matter-of-fact and business-like, but also extremely thorough. Before departing, he told me that I was to ring his dispatch office whenever I was planning to leave the building, and two men would be assigned to watch over me until I returned.

Chapter 11

~ *Yakov* ~

Yakov came to see me that afternoon. "I heard what happened to you this morning," he said, hitching his bottom onto the edge of my desk and taking one of my hands in his, studying the grazes on my palms and knuckles from my fall. "Are you all right?"

I nodded, smiling at his concern for my welfare. "It left me shaking afterwards, what with it being a surprise, and the ferocity of the attack, but the strange thing is that I was sure I would survive."

He smiled. "I am amazed that you are relatively unhurt."

"Ah," I said ruefully, "not completely." I cast a quick eye at the door, to make sure it was closed, then pulled up my skirt as far as my knees, to reveal a matching pair of blood-stained bandages. As I did so, I realised that it was a rather wild and abandoned thing to do, to expose my legs to a man, but he was a good friend, and I felt comfortable in his company. "I scraped them while crawling on the path after falling through the gate," I explained. His eyes opened wide. He tried to pretend it was in shock at my wounds, but I could see that he was also enjoying the sight of my bare limbs.

Suppressing a grin, I lowered my skirt again while he gathered his flustered wits.

"I ... erm ... wondered if you would like a little distraction," he said, rather too quickly. "An evening at the ballet. Alexander Gorsky, the director at the Bolshoi, is a good friend, and I can easily get tickets at short notice."

"What a good idea," I exclaimed. "I haven't been to the ballet for years."

"I think you'll love it. Gorsky has his own ideas, and has changed Swan Lake in a way that I think is good, but which many of the critics hate. Well, like so many people, they can't deal with change. What do you say? Will you come tonight?"

"Thank you, Yakov, I would love to."

"Splendid," he smiled, jumping from my desk and kissing my hand before releasing it and heading for the door. "I am off out now. I'll return and pick you up here at seven."

* * *

After he had left, I looked despondently down at my dress. Chosen to be plain and sturdy for work, it was also now grubby, scuffed and blood-stained from my adventure. Certainly not suitable for the ballet. The big clock on my wall told me that I had less than three hours to get ready. I dashed through to Aleksandra's office. "Where can I get a dress suitable for the ballet?" I said, breathlessly.

"Was that Yakov's voice I heard?" she asked, mischievously.

"Were you listening at the door?" I countered, grinning. "You were!" I pointed at her, accusingly.

"No! Certainly not!" But there was a guilty expression on her face. "Oh, very well. He came to see me first, to seek my advice. He didn't know if you would accept. I said that there was only one way to find out, and that was for him to ask you himself." She paused. "I wasn't listening, though, honestly."

I laughed. "Oh, I wouldn't mind if you had."

She stood up from her desk. "Come with me to my apartment," she instructed, "and let's see if we can find something suitable for you to wear."

She abandoned her desk, and I followed her along the corridor to the stairs that led up to the third-floor rooms. Not for her the ostentation of the Kremlin Palace like Lenin and Stalin, she was happy with a modest, but still comfortable, apartment above her office.

I suspected that these rooms had once been provided for the minor royals and flunkies who formed part of the various Tsars' retinues over the centuries ~ the dukes and duchesses, barons and earls, cousins, high-ranking military officers and honoured retainers who helped to keep the monarchy afloat. Aleksandra had a suite of three rooms, and she led me through an elegant lounge into her bedroom.

There she opened up her wardrobe, revealing a row of beautiful gowns. Seeing my amazement, she grinned. "I have expensive tastes when it comes to clothes," she said, lifting out one. "Try this, I think it will suit you." It was a beautiful, modern dress, of soft, creamy satin that seemed to flow in layers, with ruffled edges of golden silk.

She helped me into it, and she was right, it fitted well, but I was rather shocked at how revealing it was. I looked at myself in her long mirror as Aleksandra adjusted the lace sleeves and pulled at the wide, silk ribbon that formed a simple belt. The neckline was low and wide, leaving my shoulders bare and a good deal of my bust exposed. From there, folds of ivory satin followed the shape of my body until they flared from the slightly-emphasized bustle to descend gracefully to the floor.

I was transported back to the night of the grand ball at Saint Catherine's Palace, two years earlier, when I had met Frederick, my young Prince. But I hardly recognised the young woman whose image I now saw in the mirror.

Through my exile and imprisonment with the royal

family over the past year, I had become accustomed to wearing simple clothes, often dirty and worn ~ now, suddenly, I was transformed into a lady again, only the lady had blossomed. I was no longer the little girl, dressing up for her first ball ~ the person who returned my stare now was a woman, with curves and care-lines and, yes, breasts. Only my knitted hat spoiled the effect; it certainly did not compliment the rest of my ensemble. Aleksandra laughed as I snatched at it and whipped it off, revealing the downy growth it hid. My hair was slowly growing back, but it was still very short, and split by the scar where the bullet had passed.

"I think a wig would be helpful," she grinned, reaching up to lift down one of several boxes ranged along the top of the wardrobe.

* * *

After a bath in Aleksandra's private bathroom, I began to look and feel better. She redressed my wounds, then helped me into the gown, completing my outfit with a pair of gloves to hide my wounded hands, a coiffed wig to conceal my shaved head, and a beautiful pair of silk slippers. I looked down at how much of my skin was exposed, and turned to look anxiously at her. She held up a finger, reached into the wardrobe, and produced a silk shawl, which she draped over my shoulders.

Yakov arrived early to pick me up, and smiled with approval when he saw my outfit. We made our way down to the yard, followed by two bodyguards. An elegant Landau was awaiting us, with a liveried driver and footman, and drawn by a pair of white horses. Yakov held my arm as I climbed the step, while the footman held open the door for us. I felt like Cinderella going to the ball, though the illusion was somewhat stretched by the presence of our two burly bodyguards standing to one side.

We arrived at the theatre as darkness began to fall. The street-lighter was going from one lamp-post to the next along the avenue beside Teatralnaya square, lighting each gas-lamp with his long pole, and, at the top of the square, the colonnaded entrance to the Bolshoi was glowing like a candle from hidden spotlights. A bronze statue of Apollo and his chariot, hovering above the entrance, shone almost magically as we alighted and began to slowly mount the wide steps.

The last time I had been to the ballet, though I could not tell Yakov, was at the Mariinsky Theatre in Saint Petersburg, four years earlier, with The Tsar and Empress and their two eldest daughters. On that occasion, I had sat with them in the royal box.

The Bolshoi Theatre proved to be just as impressive, with thick red carpets, gold-and-blue painted ceilings, marble columns and golden cherubs. We were enthusiastically welcomed at the door by Yakov's friend, the Ballet Master, Alexander Gorsky, who accompanied us to the seats he had reserved. I was shocked when, after climbing plush stairs, we emerged above the theatre between velvet drapes ~ once again I was in a royal box.

We sat, and Gorsky remained with us for a while, chatting as the orchestra tuned up and the audience began to fill the theatre, before excusing himself to attend to other matters. I saw heads turn as patrons scrutinised the new royalty, and heard whisperings as they drew their conclusions. I was embarrassed, and would have preferred the relative anonymity of a stalls seat, or perhaps a regular box. But I was determined to enjoy my evening and not be put off by the ostentation and the gossiping.

I was not disappointed. When the lights went down and the performance began, I was regaled by Tchaikovsky's beautiful music and the stunning dancing of Yekaterina Geltzer and the Bolshoi company ~ it was a delight for me from start to finish. However, not everyone felt the same, and there were some loud mutterings of discontent from the stalls during the performance ~ as Yakov had told me, some patrons did not like the changes Gorsky had made to the 'usual' way things were done. A few people even marched out indignantly before the end, but not many, and there were cheers and thunderous applause at the conclusion.

* * *

Afterwards, we stopped outside my apartment, with our escort keeping respectfully out of sight around the corner in the stairway.

"I've had a lovely time, thank you Yakov," I said. "Just what I needed to forget what happened this morning."

He smiled and gently held my hand, then surprised me by suddenly leaning forward and kissing me on the lips. It was not passionate, but it was tender and lingering, his moustache slightly scratchy on my skin. "I hope it will be the first of many," he said, softly.

I was flustered, it had happened so quickly, so unexpectedly. "I hope so too," I answered. "But, Yakov, I cannot ... " I didn't know what to say, how to tell him that I was not available, that I had a past he would not like. "I am ... my life is ... complicated," I eventually managed to blurt out.

He looked disappointed. "I am sorry," he said, quickly. "How selfish of me; I am rushing you; you have been through so much, and you hardly know me." He lifted my hand to his lips, and kissed my fingers. "I will see you tomorrow at work."

I kept hold of his hand, so that, when he turned to go, he

had to stop. "It's not what you think," I said, smiling. "I hope that I can explain, soon. You are a lovely man, and a good friend. I would really like to go out with you again."

Explain what? That I was a niece of the Tsar? That I barely escaped with my life when Nicholas and his family were murdered by the Bolsheviks? How could I possibly tell him?

Chapter 12

~ *Friday 9 August 1918* ~

The next day, Friday, mid-morning, I knocked on the door from my office to Yakov's and walked in, as had become our routine, with his tea and toast on a tray. I was smiling in recollection of our pleasant evening together, and looking forward to some friendly conversation. Unexpectedly, though, he had a guest, and their heads turned towards me in unison. A smile began to form on Yakov's face, and he rose to introduce me, but I had already recognised his guest, and he had recognised me.

"Well, if it isn't the uppity little lady's maid!" A sneer spread across Yurovsky's face as he turned back to Yakov. "What's she doing here?"

I was frozen to the spot, my mind racing. Yakov's head was turning from me to Yurovsky and back to me, a look of surprise on his face. "She's my secretary," he said, slowly. "How do you know her?"

There was no escape for me, so I walked over to his desk and put the tray in a space at one end, avoiding eye contact with Yurovsky, then stepped behind it and stood beside Yakov to face the onslaught that I knew was coming.

Yurovsky laughed. "She hasn't told you? Now, why does that not surprise me? Miss Tereshchenko and I are old friends, aren't we, Natalie?"

"Hardly friends," I retorted, huffily.

"What is going on here?" Yakov asked, turning to me, his face a mixture of confusion and rising anger.

"It's true," I replied, desolately. "My name is Natalie

Tereshchenko. I met comrade Yurovsky in Tobolsk, earlier this year, when he took over custody of the ex-Tsar and his family; I used to work for them as a Lady in Waiting."

Yakov stared at me for what felt like a lifetime. I didn't know what to say or do, I couldn't meet his eyes, and stared instead at the floor. Eventually, he turned back to Yurovsky. "Will you please excuse us, Comrade? My secretary and I need to talk."

Grinning, Yurovsky nodded, bowed slightly at the waist, and left. As the outer door closed, Sverdlov glared at me. Then, without a word, he stood up from his desk and walked through the still-open doorway into my office. He disappeared from my sight as he crossed the room, but I heard him open Aleksandra's door, and heard his voice. Then, a moment later, they came back together.

Yakov returned to his desk, and Aleksandra stood in the doorway, a puzzled expression on her face. I was still standing beside his chair, had not moved.

"Tell her what you just told me," Yakov barked at me.

Miserably, I repeated it. I was terrified. Yakov's anger was almost physical, his hands were closed tightly into fists on the desk before him, his mouth tight, his lips white. Aleksandra's face was unreadable.

"Are you a spy for the Whites?" Sverdlov asked, his voice trembling.

"No!" I answered quickly, shaking my head vigorously. "I am on your side." I turned to Aleksandra. "I'm sorry I didn't tell you; I was afraid for my life."

"Do you think we are such brutes?" she said, simply.

I shook my head. "I know now that you are not." I said, then pointed to the door through which Yurovsky had left. "But he is, and I had no way of knowing, when we met, that you were not the same."

"So you let me make a fool of myself," Yakov said.

I looked from one to the other; I didn't know how to show them how much they meant to me.

"I didn't intend to, honestly. At first, I thought it would be just a job, I didn't expect to get close to anyone, to really care as I do for both of you. Over time, as we have become friends, I have been trying to find a way to break the news, but couldn't find the right time. Will you let me tell you now, so you can understand?"

Aleksandra took the few steps needed to bring her to my side, then led me by the arm to the chairs before Yakov's desk. She sat in the one vacated by Yurovsky, and I lowered my trembling body into the other.

Hesitantly, at first, I recounted my years with the royal family, described my work, my feelings about them, and my antipathy towards their power. Of course, I carefully omitted to reveal my own royal blood ~ somehow, I felt that it would be one fact too many.

I told them about our exile and imprisonment. My voice faltered when I recalled the carnage of that night in Yekaterinburg. "I was there, in that house, when Nicholas and Alexandra and all their children were murdered by the butcher Avadeyev and his men, on Lenin's orders. That is why I was afraid to tell you before. My friends, innocent servants, were also slaughtered. Yurovsky was there, complicit in the murder."

I paused, studying them. I sensed some sympathy in Aleksandra's face, and Yakov's expression had changed, his eyes had opened a little wider, as though he was seeing something unexpected. I thought he was beginning to understand, until I resumed my account and told them about Max ~ then I saw his jaw tighten and his mouth again squeeze tightly closed. I forced myself to ignore it, and pressed on.

"Max helped me to avoid the shooting and flee from the

house. Avadeyev has been trying since that night to find me. We caught a train, hoping to flee to England, where I thought we would be safe, but Max was injured in a struggle with one of Avadeyev's men, and we had to get off again at Nizhny. After a doctor had removed the bullet, we separated to be less conspicuous. I travelled to Moscow with the nuns, and Max joined the travelling circus, which was also supposed to be coming to Moscow."

And then I reached the moment in my account when I described my attempt to end my life outside the convent. "I knew that Avadeyev wanted me for what I knew, and I saw soldiers massing outside the convent. I put the facts as I knew them together, and thought they were there to arrest me. Knowing what Avadeyev is capable of, I decided it was better to let them kill me."

"But, instead, the soldiers were there to close the convent," Aleksandra was nodding. "Natalie, we knew nothing about you. Our friend Yurovsky and his associate Avadeyev, have managed to keep your escape a secret." She turned to Sverdlov, who was also nodding, though his expression was still grim, and his eyes stabbed at me like flashes of lightening.

"A little honesty would have been nice," he said, petulantly, after a pause.

I could understand why he was hurt and jealous, but I was also angry that he dismissed my fears without seeing my point of view. "Oh yes," I retorted, "that's easy for you to say. I'm just trying to stay alive in a country that wants to see me dead ~ and none of it is my fault. Can you honestly say that you would have accepted me, in the beginning, if I had told you who I really am?"

"I would have liked the chance to," he replied.

I glared at him. "Well, it wouldn't have been your neck on the block, would it?"

Aleksandra held up her hands. "Enough, already. Natalie is right. Having heard her story, I can understand why she preferred to adopt a new persona. The question is: what are we going to do now?"

I looked from one to the other. "Please don't hand me over to Avadeyev, he is a sadist. If you want to kill me, just do it quickly."

Aleksandra stood, suddenly, her head down. "You really think we are all evil, don't you?" she said, quietly. "And who can blame you, after what you have seen." She cast a glance at Sverdlov, who refused to meet her eyes. There was something in her look, and in his reticence, that told of secrets I did not know.

I rose to my feet and moved to her side. Her head was down; I thought she could even be crying. "Until I met you," I said, "I had known only one side of the revolution; and it was brutal. I'm sorry, I know now that you are not like them." I reached out a hand and brushed her arm. 'I have grown to love you as a friend, and admire you for what you do." She took my hand in hers, and held it tightly.

I turned to Sverdlov. "Yakov, I do like you very much, and I wanted to tell you everything. I'm sorry."

He shrugged; but though he didn't speak, I had a feeling he was softening a little.

Aleksandra sucked in a deep breath through her nose, then blew it out slowly between pursed lips. She was back in control.

"This is not necessarily a bad thing," she said, assertively, to Sverdlov. "Perhaps we can even make some propaganda out of it."

"But Avadeyev ... " I began.

"Avadeyev is a throwback to the Mongols, an animal. Leave him to me." Yakov interrupted.

"But he was acting on Lenin's orders." The words were out before I could stop them. Was this really me speaking? Why could I not think before opening my mouth? I had never been that bold, that rash, before. Somehow, my experiences over the past year had made me more confrontational, and this was not really the best time to bring out that trait.

"Yes, that is true," he replied, "and there were good reasons, believe me."

Aleksandra spoke again, returning to her point. "The first part of the revolution is over," she resumed, speaking to me again. "But now we are bogged down in civil war. The Whites have a powerful resistance movement, with help from abroad. They fight us unceasingly, many people are dying unnecessarily, they are holding up food supplies, and our economy cannot recover until all citizens are united."

"And you think that a convert from the Tsar's household could give the proletariat a stronger reason to fight?" I said, incredulously.

She laughed. "Well, that may be hoping for a little too much. But, perhaps, if the people saw you working with us, they may be less likely to believe the Whites' propaganda."

Suddenly, the door to the office burst open, and a big man, wearing a military uniform and sporting a large moustache, barged in. It was my first encounter with Joseph Vissarionovich Stalin.

Chapter 13

~ Stalin ~

"Ah, Joseph," said Aleksandra, coldly, "I wondered how long it would be before we saw you. And Comrade Yurovsky, what a surprise." Yurovsky was lurking in the doorway behind Stalin, smirking.

Stalin was a giant of a man, tall, broad-shouldered and barrel-chested. He had a mass of black hair and a wide, bushy moustache. He wore a smartly tailored uniform, adorned with medals.

He glared at Aleksandra for a moment, without speaking, then at me, then turned to Yakov. "This time you have gone too far, Sverdlov," he bellowed. "I have called an immediate emergency meeting of the Council. You are to attend." Then he pointed a finger at me. "And bring her with you!" Then he spun on his heels and departed, practically mowing down the still-grinning Yurovsky, who gave me a cheery wave as he closed the door behind them.

Suddenly my secret past was common knowledge, and I feared that I was living my last hours. My life was in the balance, and I had only two people to speak for me. But there was one small blessing: yes, they had found out that I used to work for the Romanovs, and that I was present at their demise, but thankfully no-one knew about my royal blood ~ that would surely have guaranteed my execution.

* * *

Together, the three of us trudged silently through busy corridors, falling into step with others heading in the same direction, presumably council members, who stared at me with blatant and hostile curiosity.

We entered the council chamber ~ a large, bright room, with windows along one side, like a row of pictures. It looked to me as though it may once have been a dining hall, in the times when the Kremlin was used by the monarch. Occupying almost the whole of the centre of the room, and running a considerable part of the length of it, was a mahogany table, where council members had already started to take their places with a scraping of plush, ornate chairs on the polished parquet floor.

I recognised Leon Trotsky, nominally the Second-in-Command to Lenin, though probably ranking no higher in the power structure than Sverdlov, taking the seat at the head of the table, asserting himself as acting Chairman. And there was Stalin, sitting with Yurovsky, about halfway down the side facing the window. I looked nervously around the room; there were no other faces I recognised. Aleksandra and Yakov led me to a chair almost opposite Stalin, and seated themselves protectively on each side of me. As more members arrived, Aleksandra whispered their names and roles to me. I tried to remember, but there were so many new faces and names, and I was so tense that I knew I would not remember them.

* * *

Trotsky tersely opened the proceedings, and, instantly, Stalin jumped to his feet, determined to say his piece before anyone else had a chance to speak.

"Comrade Stalin," announced the acting chairman, dryly.

"I want to know why we have an alien in our midst," Stalin began, hotly, pointing at me, his thick moustache quivering as he repeatedly pursed his lips. "Comrades Sverdlov and Kollontai have compromised our security by

94

bringing a refugee from the privileged classes here into the seat of our government! How did it happen? And what is more, what are we going to do about it?"

He sat down again, glaring across the table at me. I looked down at my hands, sensing all the eyes in the room turning to me, heard the hiss of their voices as they exchanged hostile whispers. I suppressed a shiver, then felt Aleksandra's hand seeking mine under the table, and I held it tightly.

To my surprise, Yakov stood and looked to the chair for recognition. "Comrade Sverdlov," Trotsky said, with a single nod of his head.

What would he say? His pride was injured, and he was still angry at me. I could only guess at the thoughts churning inside his head. My life was in his hands, and his hands were shaking.

"Comrade Chairman," he said. "Brothers." He paused, looking up and down the table, waiting for them to settle. When he had their attention, he began, and managed to shock the whole room, including me. "What, exactly, is the problem?" he asked, holding his hands out in a shrugging gesture.

Stalin's mouth fell open, and there were gasps around the room. I looked up at Yakov; his lips were white, but he managed to sound confident as he continued. "So my secretary used to work for the Tsar. Does that make her complicit in his crimes? No! It makes her as much a victim as any other citizen. In the time we have worked together I have seen her enthusiasm for our cause. She is not a spy for the Whites, I stake my name on it. She has already served Comrade Kollontai well as an assistant, happy to do the most menial work. I say, give her a chance. Who knows, having an ex-servant of the royals on our team could even be an asset."

He sat down without looking at me. I could read nothing in his face.

Stalin was on his feet in a flash, before Yakov was even in his seat, and launched into a tirade without waiting for Trotsky to recognise him.

"Give her a chance?" he spluttered, looking around at the other commissars, indignantly. "An asset?" His eyes flashed at me, and again he pointed across the table at the three of us. "A liability is what we will get!"

He held up his left hand, fingers extended, and began to pinch each one in turn with the finger and thumb of his right hand as he counted off his objections:

The thumb: "What is she going to be? A secretary? Privy to every secret that the Whites would love to know? And why is she needed? Comrades Sverdlov and Kollontai were managing perfectly well on their own before ~ why do they suddenly need an assistant now?"

Next his index finger was gripped: "In view of her past, how can we trust her? For all of Comrade Sverdlov's confidence, she could still prove to be a White spy in our midst." Again, that hostile stare.

Second finger: "What experience does she have? Nothing but the privilege of the royal household. We were all part of the revolution, risking our lives, while she sat in luxury in Alexander Palace, serving every whim of the decadent Romanovs."

Ring finger: "She's a slip of a girl. Who can take her seriously? Certainly not me!" He glared at me with a self-satisfied twitch of his shoulders.

Little finger: "And she's another woman! This chamber will soon be crawling with women! How many more?" He grinned up and down the table. "Are we being infiltrated by the gentle sex?" There were sniggers from one or two of the men. Stalin spread his arms wide. "Soon there will be no room for the men to get on with the real business of the country!"

Beaming at his own humour, he sat down, accompanied by loud laughter from around the room. I remembered Aleksandra telling me that Joe hated the idea of women being involved in government, and had always made life as difficult as possible for her.

Aleksandra raised her hand, and Trotsky acknowledged it with a nod. "Comrade Kollontai, your reply," he said loudly into the babble of voices.

Aleksandra stood.

"Another woman?" She fixed Stalin with one of her glares. He held it, unblinking. "Well, women constitute half the population," she continued, "so why should it be a problem that there are now two of us on the Women's Commissariat? Two! It is hardly an invasion, is it? And, in case it escaped your attention, comrades, you men did not fight the revolution alone ~ women marched beside you from the start, played a vital role. Women from the factories and the shops. Women died beside you for the cause. It could not have happened without us. I, too, have spent time in the Tsar's prisons, as have many unsung heroines of the fight for freedom."

She paused to let her words sink in, then shocked me. "I would like Comrade Tereshchenko to reply on her own behalf," she said, and sat down again. The room fell into stunned silence.

Me? I looked at her, and she nodded. Nervously I rose to my feet.

Aware that my voice had to carry to the far ends of the table, I tried to add power to it, and heard a strident tone to my first words. "Comrade Stalin is right, on all counts," I began. "I am small, and young, and inexperienced." I softened the tone as best I could, while still trying to project to the farthest seats. "And why should you trust me? As far as you can see, I have done little so far to earn that trust. I would like to carry on, to prove myself, but for that I need you to take a risk and give me a chance."

I smiled, trying to lighten the atmosphere, but it was a weak, tight smile, and was not returned by the hard faces that lined the table like a jury waiting to pass sentence. I paused for a second to lock eyes with Stalin, forced myself to look at him, though my legs were shaking like reeds in a gale. He met my gaze, but did not respond; his face was a mask.

Flustered and lost for words, I again looked around the room. A drone of male voices had started. Many of them did not appear to be listening for what I had to say, they were leaning towards each other in twos and threes, talking, discussing me. I needed their attention, my life depended on it. I sought Trotsky's eyes; he at least was following me. He banged the table with his little wooden hammer to get their attention. "Comrades!" he called loudly. "The chair recognises this speaker, please have the courtesy to listen." He nodded encouragingly to me.

I sent him a smile of thanks while I gathered my wits.

"I served the Romanovs because it was the only life I knew," I resumed into the relative silence. "But that does not mean that I was oblivious to their faults, though I was ignorant of the events taking place beyond the palace walls, and not privy to their secrets. Since working with my colleagues here, I have learnt something of the crimes committed by the Tsar, and I can tell you that I hate them for what they did. I do not deserve to be blamed for the actions of those who dominated me as they dominated Russia, and I sincerely want to help this council in whatever little way I am able."

Finally, I gave in to my trembling legs, and almost fell

back into my chair, aware that I had just addressed the most important men in the country. Again I felt Aleksandra's hand reach for mine under the table.

Of course, I was not permitted to remain for the rest of the meeting, when my fate would be decided, and Aleksandra was no longer a council member, so she led me to the door. Though she kept a serious expression as we crossed the room, when we reached the door and her face was hidden from all except me, she gave me a big wink. "Well done," she mouthed.

Chapter 14

~ *Lenin* ~

Aleksandra and I went to the canteen, a huge dining hall on the ground floor, and collected a pot of tea, then carried it upstairs and waited in her office for Sverdlov to return with the result of the council vote.

"Thank you for supporting me," I said as I closed the door.

"I hope I am not making a big mistake," she replied. "Yakov and I are sticking our necks out, here, and we really know nothing about you. I am relying purely on my instinct; it has never let me down before, but this has happened too quickly for my comfort."

"Your instinct is right, I am sincere," I said.

We sat, and I took a sip of my drink, noticing as I did so that my hands were still trembling. "What will happen to me if the council votes against us?" I asked.

"I don't like to think about that," she said. "Joseph will probably demand that we hand you over to him."

I knew what that meant. Stalin and Avadeyev were two of a kind. I could not expect clemency.

"Natalie, how did you come to be working for the Empress?" she suddenly asked. The question I had been dreading.

"My father died when I was little; I never knew him," I told her. That was true, though it would not do to mention who my father was. "My mother could not cope alone, and, as she worked for the Empress as a seamstress, she asked for her help. Alexandra took me in, fed and clothed me, and put me to work as a maid."

"But you rose to become a Lady In Waiting. Not many servants get that kind of opportunity ~ it is usually reserved for members of the royal family."

I nodded. "Yes, but it was a small household at Alexander palace, and I was always willing to work hard. Most of my time was with Tatiana. She was pleased with what I did, and when she needed an assistant, she asked for me."

"What became of your mother?"

"She never came to see me, the whole of my childhood. I was told that she moved away."

"And how did you come to be with the family in exile?"

I shrugged. "I had nowhere else to go, no other family. My only real friends, two of the maids I grew up with, were going with the family, so I went too."

At that moment, Sverdlov burst in through the door. "Ah, there you are," he said, flopping down on Aleksandra's settee. He looked happier, though still tense. "We carried it ... just ... thirteen to twelve, with the chairman's vote. Stalin is livid!"

He seemed to be more pleased about scoring a win over Stalin than about saving my life.

* * *

Later that same day, I was carrying messages down to the telegraph office when a crowd of security men rushed past me, shouting at me to get out of their way. When I reached the clerk at the desk, I asked what was going on. "Lenin has returned early from his diplomatic trip to Germany," he informed me.

On my return to the office, I passed the information on to Yakov. Since the council vote, I had felt an easing in the atmosphere between us, but the warmth was gone.

"You can bet that Yurovsky and Stalin will make a point

of informing him about you," he said, grimly.

And so it was. Within an hour, I found myself walking across the square and along a tree-lined avenue to the Kremlin Palace, the stunning building that had once been the occasional home of generations of Tsars. I had been summoned to visit Lenin in his quarters, and was accompanied by his secretary, Vladimir Dmitriyevich Bonch-Bruevich, and two soldiers.

"He wants to meet you personally," Bonch-Bruevich explained as we walked. "Normally, he would not be concerned with minor appointments such as this within the various Commissariats, but your background makes you special ~ something of a threat, and something of an enigma."

"My life is an enigma, comrade Bonch-Bruevich," I said with a shrug as we marched briskly beneath trees bright with pink and white blossoms. "The accident of my previous employment hangs around my neck like a sign saying 'Unclean!'"

He smiled, mirthlessly, as I imagined the angel of death might smile. A tall, stocky man, with a heavy beard, and dressed all in black, Bonch-Bruevich looked more like a rabbi than secretary to the leader of Russia.

"It is his purpose to ensure that you are not bringing The Plague into our midst," he commented. It was almost a joke ~ almost ~ but was, perhaps more likely, an accusation.

We entered the palace by the main doors, Bonch-Bruevich receiving a salute from the soldiers guarding the entrance, and began to mount the elegant staircase.

"You will address him as 'Comrade Ilyich'," he informed me as he strode up the wide, marble steps.

It sounded so much like a royal command that I stopped climbing and looked at him in amazement.

"What?" he asked, irritably, also pausing astride two steps and looking back down at me.

"Not 'Your majesty'?" I mocked.

His beard twitched. "Don't be ridiculous," he grunted, turning and strutting to the top of the stairs, then marching ahead without waiting for me.

I refused to run to keep up with him, and walked steadily, the yards building up between us, until he stopped at a door, where he had to wait for me. Looking impatiently over his shoulder until I arrived, he eventually knocked, and after a voice spoke from beyond, opened the door and held it for me. "Comrade Natalie Tereshchenko," he announced.

* * *

'Ah, Comrade Ilyich, how good of you to see me.'

I didn't say that, of course, but the rogue thought raced through my mind, and I had to fight back a nervous grin as I walked into his office. He looked up and gestured wordlessly to the chair before his desk, then continued writing. As I crossed the room on the thick blue carpet, I looked around me at the luxurious décor, similar to that with which I had grown up in Alexander Palace but, if anything, even grander. When I reached the chair, I sat in it and waited for him to acknowledge me.

He sat upright as he worked, immaculately dressed in a dark suit, with a waistcoat and tie, his beard neatly groomed, his bald head shining. When he felt that he had kept me waiting long enough, he put down his pen and skewered me with a piercing stare.

"Socialism is not something you can just take up as a hobby," he began, cuttingly. "It is not a passing tram, on which to jump when your motor car has broken down. Why do you think we should take you in, now that you no longer have royal masters to serve?"

I watched him speaking, I noticed that, though his mouth moved to release the sounds, there was no expression on his face. It was odd ~ his eyes were sharp, watchful, yet telling nothing; I could not sense the soul behind them.

I thought carefully before answering:

"Like every child, Comrade, I did not choose where I was brought up or who my parents were. I was placed with the royals as a charity case, when my own mother could not support me. My status in the royal household was no better than any of the other servants. Your analogy falls down on one thing: the motor car was never mine, I did not even ride in it. My place was to run beside it, pandering to the passengers. They kept us ignorant or misinformed about the true state of the nation, and it is only since I have been working with Comrade Kollontai that I have discovered what was really happening."

I stopped, consciously holding back from saying any more, aware that I could fall into the trap of pleading my case, and determined not to be intimidated into doing so. I knew that they did not all agree on my role within the party ~ Stalin had already shown his hostility unambiguously ~ but I was no longer the timid servant girl, I would argue but not beg. His eyebrows twitched a little.

"These are dangerous times," he said. "Are you prepared to die for the cause?"

"I believe I have already proved that." I replied, simply, removing my knitted hat and pointing to the scar on my forehead.

"Ah yes, your ... um ... exposure at the convent." Was that a hint of a smile? "I have Captain Sergeyev's report here." He held it up as if to prove the point. "Very well,

Miss Tereshchenko, go, with my approval. I will be interested to see if our experiment bears any fruit."

He stood, and extended his hand across the desk. It was a surprising gesture, and I accepted the handshake with a smile and a small curtsey. He did not smile back, but I thought I detected a slight twinkle in his eyes as I turned to leave.

He still had one more surprise for me. As I reached the door and turned the golden knob, I heard him add, quietly, but loud enough for me to know that I was meant to hear: "Watch out for Stalin."

I turned to look back at him, but his head was down, his eyes on his work, not on me. It was as though I had imagined that he had said it, though I knew I had not.

Chapter 15

~ *Tuesday 13th August 1918* ~

A large, red sun was disappearing behind the ragged skyline of roofs and spires of Moscow when I walked home after another long, busy day. One of my escorts for the night, Leo, walked beside me, chatting, as though we were old friends (it was an act, of course) while the other, Stanislav, ambled watchfully a few feet behind ~ to all appearances, just another pedestrian, looking in shop windows.

When we had climbed the stairs and reached my apartment, I was about to put my key in the lock when Leo stopped me with a hand on my arm. Wordlessly, he twitched his nose, and I obediently sniffed the air. Cigarette smoke, faint but certain. Stanislav took my key from my trembling fingers, and with a gesture of his head indicated that I should move away. I retreated down the corridor while the two men took position, one on each side of the door.

Pressed against the wall, Stanislav stretched out an arm and inserted my key in the lock and turned it. I saw Leo remove his jacket as Stanislav pushed the door open, then … nothing happened. After a nod from Stanislav, Leo threw his jacket across the open face of the doorway towards his partner, and the silence was shattered by a burst of gunshots, deafening in the confines of the corridor. The jacket jerked in mid-flight, landing on the floor between the two men, and plaster spurted from the wall opposite. At the same instant, I saw Stanislav's arm swing in a short arc as he tossed something in through the open doorway. Both men took a step backwards, and instinctively I too moved further away.

I reached the stairs, and jumped when I found that there was a man standing on the top step. He held a finger up to his lips, and flapped his other hand, telling me to pass him and go down the stairs. I had three escorts, not two! As I obeyed, I heard a loud thud from behind me, and stopped, looking over my shoulder.

"Smoke grenade," the man said. "We want to take him alive, whoever he is."

He stepped out into the corridor, a pistol in his hand, to give his companions support, but no more shots were fired. I heard violent coughing as, presumably, the intruder or intruders staggered out of my flat into the arms of my escorts.

I joined the third man on the landing, and saw my protectors dragging someone along the corridor towards me, away from the fumes that were billowing from my door. He was middle-aged, balding, with a brown moustache and wearing rough, working clothes. He was still coughing and struggling in great gulps to regain his breath.

As they handcuffed him, Leo told me that I would not be able to enter my apartment until the air had cleared and the place had been checked for clues. So, after Stanislav had locked the door, I accompanied them and their captive through the evening gloom, back to the Kremlin, with their mysterious colleague again trailing behind. Now that I knew there was a third man protecting me, I could see how he had kept station not far away, while remaining inconspicuous.

The man they had apprehended was not the youth who had tried to crush me with his motor car a few days earlier ~ this man was older and bigger, with heavy eyebrows, like a gorilla. We received some strange looks from passers-by as my companions marched on either side of him, his wrists bound behind his back with handcuffs. We parted company at the garrison, they taking their prisoner upstairs to their mysterious Department Thirteen for interrogation, I to return to my office.

I found Aleksandra still at work, and told her what had happened. She helped me to arrange for some workmen with gas-masks to open up my flat the next day, then she gave me some blankets, and I fashioned a bed in the corner of my office for the night.

"Where is Department Thirteen?" I asked her afterwards.

"That's Stalin's baby, on the top floor," she replied. "You're not thinking of going there, are you?"

I nodded. "I want to find out who's trying to kill me," I answered grimly.

"You won't be allowed up there without a special pass," she said. "And knowing what dear Joseph thinks of you, I wouldn't fancy your chances of him signing one."

She picked up her phone.

"Hello Natasha," she said into the mouthpiece after a brief pause. "Are you still on duty?" She laughed at the reply, then asked for Department Thirteen, gesturing for me to stand beside her, and tilting the earpiece so I could hear what was said.

"Yes?" came a tinny voice, like a gramophone record.

"Kollontai," she said. "Comrade Tereshchenko's agents brought in a suspect this evening. Do you have any news?"

"Hold on," said the disembodied voice.

We waited, and eventually a new voice came cracking from the machine. "Agent Solovyov. Tell her that he is refusing to give any information and had no identification with him. I doubt we will have anything to report before morning."

Aleksandra thanked him and replaced the earpiece in its little cradle, ending the call.

"I wouldn't want to be their prisoner," she said quietly, sending a shiver up my spine.

* * *

After a restless night on the floor of my office, in which my mind kept replaying the dramatic events outside my flat, and comparing them with the earlier attempt on my life, I woke with the dawn and folded up my blankets, dressed, then stood for a few minutes at my window looking pensively down at the stable-hands working in the yard below. The grooms led each horse out in turn, and brushed them down while boys cleaned out the pen. Steam rose into the cool dawn air from the heap of soiled straw growing in their wheelbarrow. When it was full, the lad ran with it across the yard and transferred the muck into a cart that was waiting to spirit it away, as though there was no such thing as smelly manure to offend the gentle people of the Kremlin.

I had a busy day ahead, but first I needed to make my flat habitable again. The specialists that I had requested arrived early, carrying protective overalls and boxes of tools, and we headed out onto the street, picking up my bodyguard of Stanislav and another agent, Vasily this time, as we went.

At the apartment, I helped the engineers put on their coveralls and gas-masks, then retreated with my guards to the far end of the corridor, while the men opened the door and entered through the errant wisps of smoke that escaped into the hallway like homeless spirits.

"The man you arrested, what have you learned?" I asked Stanislav as we waited.

He looked uncomfortable. "He refused to speak, would not tell us his name or why he was here. We have handed him over to the Special Investigations Office to see if they can get anything. They have ... methods." He shrugged his shoulders, then looked down at his feet.

"Torture?" I said, shocked. "You mean they will torture him, don't you?"

He nodded.

"I don't want that! What can I do to get him back? I won't have a man tortured in my name."

"We cannot release him," he said, defiantly, raising his eyes to my face. "He fired at government agents, it is an official matter now."

I found that I was trembling as my imagination conjured up awful images of what could be happening to the poor man. I tried to convince myself that it was no more or less than he deserved ~ he had set out to kill me, after all. I failed, as he had failed.

Ten minutes later the engineers emerged with their masks dangling on their chests. I thanked them as they peeled off their coveralls, then I entered my flat and looked around. There seemed to be little damage, apart from a hole burned in the rug where the smoke canister had erupted; I would have to replace that. The windows were open, but the oily smell of smoke was still quite strong, and would probably take a long time to dissipate.

I thanked the engineers again as they departed, then Stanislav, Vasily and I started to check my room to see if anything had been stolen. With so few possessions, that didn't take long ~ there was nothing missing, and the intruder had not left any clues.

We closed the windows, and were soon walking back to the Kremlin; I had a favour to ask my boss.

Chapter 16

~ *Wednesday 14th August 1918* ~

Nervously, I opened the door that joined my office to Aleksandra's. "Can you spare a minute?" I asked as she raised her head from the pile of letters she was reading.

She waved me in, leaning back in her chair and stretching. "What's up?"

"I need to go to Nizhny Novgorod," I said, taking a seat opposite her.

"Sure, we can arrange that, but why?"

"I have to find out what has happened to Max," I explained, "starting from the day he joined the circus. At the moment, my head is in turmoil, wondering why and how he has disappeared and where he could be. I don't even know if he is still alive."

"Do you want some time off work?"

"Yes, please. Just a few days."

She was thoughtful for a moment, then leaned over her desk and rifled through some papers, drawing out one and passing it over to me. It was the schedule for her upcoming 'agitational' trip that we had been organizing, to meet and encourage the workers in the textile mills.

"You can accompany me as far as Orekhovo, then break off on your own to Nizhny. I would like you to help me by stopping off at Kovrov to check the engineering works and the mill ~ I am sure the managers there are working a deal to cream off the profits ~ and you could address a meeting for me in Nizhny, but once that is done your time will be your own for the rest of the week, and we will both arrive back here at about the same time. How does that sound?"

I grinned. "Perfect. I knew you would come up with something."

"Right. We will print some posters and leaflets, to make it official; you will be my representative. And you will need a military escort."

"Military?" I exclaimed.

She nodded. "Yes, a visible deterrent and a sign of your authority."

I sighed. "I suppose so."

"Four men should be enough, in addition to the agents from Department Thirteen."

I thought for a moment. "There is a women's regiment, is there not?"

Again she nodded. "The First Petrograd Women's Battalion. Trotsky wants them disbanded, but I have managed to keep them active."

"Then I would like my escort to be women soldiers. It will be a sign to everyone that we have a real role in the new system."

"I like that," she grinned. "Send a telegram to their commander, asking for volunteers."

* * *

Aleksandra started teaching me all I would need to know for the trip. It was a huge task to undertake in such a short time. So much new information was bombarding me that I quickly realised I could not hope to remember it all, and began to carry a notebook in which I constantly scribbled as much as I could. Every evening, in my apartment, I sat beyond midnight, reading through my notes and re-writing them into an exercise book, to reinforce them in my mind.

Aleksandra's mission was to talk to the women in the textile mills and factories, to encourage them, stir them up, keep their support alive for the fledgling communist government. These were the women who had built the fire of the revolution in 1905, and had marched the streets in large numbers in 1917, playing a significant role in toppling the royal family from power. Aleksandra regarded them as sisters.

At each stage of our preparations for the trip, she briefed me on the background to it, the history and politics of the revolution, and of the textile industry. I began to understand why the mill-workers had become a major factor in spearheading the revolution ~ when the exploitation of men, women and children by wealthy mill owners, the dreadful working conditions, and the lack of regulations to protect the workers, finally pushed them into rebellion.

"The Tsar conspired with the industrialists," she told me. "They supported him while their wealth grew, and the poor were the source of that wealth, a resource to be exploited and suppressed. He made sure that the Dumas did not pass any new laws to stifle profits, and he was encouraged in it by the Empress and spurred on by Rasputin."

"Rasputin?" I said, incredulously. "I knew he had them under his spell, but I had no idea he was involved in matters of state."

She crossed the room to a cabinet, and rummaged for a minute, returning with a wad of papers. "Here," she said grimly, "read these."

I quickly scanned the first few. They were copies of messages sent between Nicholas and Alexandra when they were apart, dated over a period from early 1916 to the end of 1917, many of them written by Nicholas from his military headquarters near the battlefront of the war against Germany. As I read the first, I saw that the royals often referred in their exchanges to 'our friend', who was advising them on everything from personal relationships to the conduct of the war against Germany. After skimming a few more pages, I lifted my head to stare in amazement at Aleksandra. "This 'friend' was Rasputin?" I asked.

She nodded, her lips pressed tightly together, her eyebrows raised.

I returned my attention to the papers, quickly flipping through them, reading random passages. "I didn't know," I said eventually. "I was there, in the palace, and I saw the casual power he held over them, but I never dreamed it extended so far."

"They were obsessed with the notion that they were chosen by their god to rule over Russia," she said. "When Rasputin arrived, they thought he had been sent by that god to guide them. He had them completely under his control, perhaps by some kind of hypnosis."

It was so obvious, now that she had told me, that I wondered aloud why I had never seen it.

"Even their closest friends did not know the real extent of his involvement," she explained with a shrug. "From what I have learned since you have been here, they told you all only as little about things as possible. Did you know that it was strongly rumoured that he regularly had sexual intercourse with, not only the Empress, but also all the daughters?"

"No!" I exclaimed. "That's not possible!" But I stopped, suddenly remembering incidents, little things that had seemed odd but insignificant at the time. Put them together, though, in the light of this latest revelation, and I could see how the stories could be true.

Aleksandra saw my expression change, and smiled grimly. "Nicholas's surviving brother, and some other members of the family, knew what was happening. That's why they conspired to kill Rasputin."

"But Maria, Tatiana, even Anastasia? She was only twelve years old!"

She nodded. "He convinced them he was doing it for their god, to fill them with heavenly seed "

I was shaking my head in shock, unable to speak.

"Take those papers home, if you like," Aleksandra said. "You can bring them back in the morning."

I did, and they gave me nightmares.

Chapter 17

~ Friday 16th August 1918 ~

Two days passed, and we received the posters from the printers for my part of the tour. It felt strange to see my face on them, headlined with the stirring message: "Women Workers for Russia!" We checked them, then split them into two bundles and sent them off to the committees in Kovrov and Nizhny.

Also, following my telegram to the Women's Battalion, I had received a list of six volunteers to join my growing security army, and I arranged to interview them all on Friday afternoon.

When the day arrived, I sat at my desk, pensively studying again the names of the girls who had applied. A familiar name had struck me when the telegram from their commandant first arrived ~ Radochka Petrov.

I grew up with the Petrov twins, Radochka and Polira, at Alexander Palace in my days as a housemaid. They were my closest friends, and we had remained together when we accompanied the royals into exile in Tobolsk. But when a chance was offered for some of us to return home I had to stay behind to care for the injured duchess Tatiana, though I insisted that Rada and Polya took the opportunity to get away to safety. We had hoped to meet up again, one day, but in my circumstances it had begun to seem very unlikely. I remembered standing tearfully at the upstairs window of the governor's mansion in Tobolsk, watching the cart carrying them to the railway station on the first leg of the long journey to their home town of Azov, and felt my eyes sting again as I recalled that day.

Now, here was her name, as a soldier of the Red Army.

Perhaps it wasn't her ~ Petrov was a common enough name ~ but it was not unlikely that she could have joined up. About two months had elapsed since we parted, and Rada certainly had many of the qualities to be a fighter (as she had proved when we dealt with the man who raped her sister Polina). Even so, when the door opened for her interview, I was half-resigned to be disappointed.

However, despite the uniform, and the incongruous cap, there was no mistaking the slim, athletic figure that entered my office, closing the door carefully behind her and turning to sweep her hand up to her cap in a perfect salute, spoilt only by a cheeky grin. I leapt from my chair and ran to embrace her, knocking her cap flying, tears suddenly pouring from my eyes. She, too, was crying as she held me close.

After a little while, we parted, and I led her to sit beside me on the chairs near the window. "You, a soldier," was all I could manage to say, staring at her familiar face, with her dark hair, cut even shorter than before.

She grinned again, spreading her arms and pushing out her chest, as though the uniform was just a fancy dress costume. "What do you think?

"It suits you, it really does. But what made you decide to join the Red Army?"

"Well, it's not easy for a woman to get a job these days ~ at least, a job that doesn't treat her as a second-class citizen ~ and I couldn't see myself becoming an obedient little wife to some man."

I laughed, shaking my head. "Certainly not! And Polya, has she joined too?"

"Oh no, she's working for the library in Azov, and has found a nice boyfriend. She's settling down."

"I'm glad, " I said sincerely, "it's what she needs."

Rada nodded. "She's living with an aunt, my mother's sister, and once I was sure she was happy, I decided to look for something exciting to do."

"I hope this assignment won't be too exciting," I grinned. "But you're on the team, if you still want it."

"You bet!" she laughed. "Someone has to keep you out of trouble."

* * *

Rada and the other three girls I chose to travel with me were billeted in the barracks that formed part of the garrison, in a room of their own. They moved in on Saturday morning, and Rada managed to obtain a pass so she could come to stay with me for the rest of the weekend. We had much to catch up on, and it was lovely to spend time together ~ just like the old days.

We had first met when she and her twin sister Polya had arrived at Alexander Palace as housemaids in 1913. They too were orphans, eleven years old to my twelve at the time, and we shared a room from then until I was elevated to the position of Lady In Waiting to the Duchess Tatiana at the beginning of 1917. The three of us had been inseparable.

There was so much news to be exchanged; we talked the whole of Saturday away. I wanted to know about her journey home from Tobolsk, but she demanded that first I tell her how I came to be working for the Communists.

The three of us had still been together, serving the ex-royals in exile, until that night when the Whites attacked the compound of the governor's mansion, trying to rescue the family. The raiding party succeeded in taking Nicholas and Alexandra, and at first it seemed they had escaped, but they were recaptured at Yekaterinburg, and all their rescuers were killed. Yurovsky, as head of the cheka responsible for us all, decided to reduce the size of the household by sending most of the servants home, but I had to stay to look after Tatiana, who had been injured during the raid.

I told Rada about the subsequent move to Yekaterinburg to join the rest of the family, about the assassination and how Max had saved me. It seemed far-fetched, as I recounted how he had plucked me from the hands of the killers, and how we had jumped onto the train as it left Yekaterinburg station; it sounded like a chapter from 'War And Peace', yet it had happened to me.

"Yurovsky is here, in the Kremlin," I informed her. "And he has told everyone who I am."

Her eyes became like saucers. "Not about your royal blood!" she blurted.

"No, thankfully," I said, pulling a face. "He doesn't know about that. But there was a terrible hoo-hah when he recognised me and went running with his tale to Stalin. Sverdlov and Aleksandra bravely stood up for me, and managed to smooth things out, but it has ruined my relationship with Yakov."

"Relationship?" she spluttered. "What have you been up to? Is one man not enough for you?"

"It's not my fault that men are falling at my feet," I laughed, then shook my head. "Nothing has happened, I am still being true to Max. Yakov likes me, and he is a good friend. I know he wanted more than just friendship, but that wasn't going to happen, even before he found out that I had lied about who I am."

Chapter 18

~ *Monday 19th August 1918* ~

Rada and I spent our two nights together in my little bed, talking and giggling the hours away before falling asleep, clinging together as we had done so often while servants at Alexander Palace.

Then on Monday morning she rejoined the other girls to escort me when Aleksandra and I attended a gathering at one of the heavy-engineering factories on the outskirts of Moscow, where Aleksandra was to deliver a speech. The meeting was also to be addressed by Lenin, the party leader. It was a chance for me to see and hear Aleksandra in action, and to learn from the great man himself. It was also an opportunity for my new security team to bond and learn to work together.

Following the incident at my flat, I had accepted that two men were best as my close protection ~ their weight and menacing expressions would, I hoped, deter anyone contemplating harming me ~ but I liked having my army girls around me, too.

Rada, of course, was one of the four uniformed guards ~ two walking ahead, two following behind, their rifles slung over their backs, pistols at their belts in polished leather holsters. She was probably the least experienced of them all, but she knew me better than anyone else, and I felt relaxed knowing that she was with me.

I had picked a sergeant to lead the troop ~ Nina Katya, a woman who had joined the regiment a year earlier, and who previously had been one of the militants who took part in the strikes and marches of February 1917 that brought about the revolution. She told me when we met, and without any dramatisation or self-praise, that she had walked up to the soldiers guarding the barracks in Petrograd on the night of February 28th, and persuaded them to mutiny ~ to bring their weapons and join the workers. It proved to be a turning point in bringing down the monarchy.

Nina was a stocky woman, muscular, taller than the others, with deep, dark eyes that were constantly alert. She directed her team with quick instructions, like throwing a handful of words to one, then to another, placing them around me as I moved slowly through the throng with Aleksandra, and the crowd around us seethed. I knew I had made a good choice in placing her in charge.

Rada seemed to respect Nina, as did Marya, her second-in-command, and they always responded quickly to every instruction. I noticed that Sonja, however ~ the fourth of the team ~ was less amenable, and sometimes slow to obey, as though she felt that she knew better. I decided to watch her and see how things developed.

The meeting was not the orderly affair I expected. An improvised stage had been erected in a corner of the warehouse, and various speakers took turns to address the crowd. But people constantly shouted from the floor, heckling the speakers and booing off anyone who didn't say what they wanted to hear. The men seemed to dislike being addressed by Aleksandra, and chanted rudely when she began to speak, but the women nearby berated them, and soon she was able to deliver her message. She spoke well, and was cheered at the end.

Lenin stood aside most of the time, waiting for his moment, not seeking out any company, not even Aleksandra's. When he eventually was called onto the stage, there was a great noise from the crowd, some cheering and clapping, but many others shouting derisory comments; I was surprised to find that he was not universally popular.

And I was disappointed with his message. It was high in rhetoric, filled with stirring phrases, but, for me at least, it had no substance. I had hoped to hear announcements about progress with reforms, encouragement for the workers, news about food supplies, but instead he talked about the international socialist movement ~ how 'our brothers' were rising up against capitalism in Germany and America ~ and ranted about war and imperialism. After a while, I found myself looking distractedly around the room, at the faces of the crowd as they listened; most seemed to be enjoying it more than I.

* * *

Lenin's speech rattled on like a runaway train, loud and powerful and fast, but with no clear purpose, and seemingly without hope of stopping. When it finally crashed, long after night had fallen, I felt nothing but a sense of relief. This man was the leader of the revolution, said to be a gifted orator, but I found his message to be nothing but moving air, it did not seize my heart. Where Aleksandra had spoken about things that mattered to the working men and women, Lenin seemed to be only interested in his plan for world-wide revolution.

He stepped down from the stage and disappeared into a crowd of enthusiastic supporters, smiling and shaking hands; some people at least were clearly happier with his message than I had been ~ perhaps I was missing something. We all lingered, meeting union officials and activists. It was, of course, Aleksandra and Lenin that people wanted to talk with, they didn't even know who I was, so I stood aside, listening and learning as they chatted and answered questions. Out of the corner of my eye, I saw my security team talking with Aleksandra's, and felt pleased that a rapport had already developed between them.

At last, Lenin broke away from the throng, heading for the exit, and we followed him after a few moments. By the time we stepped outside into the yard, he had reached his car, and was talking animatedly with a small group of workers. It was a still, warm night, the yard was half lit by a few gas lamps that leaked yellow puddles around their feet, and the milling crowd was in good spirits, a buzz of voices floated on the calm night air.

Then, like a scene from an opera, I heard a woman's voice call out from the crowd, followed by a sudden bright flash in the gloom and the crack of a gunshot, quickly repeated. I turned to see who it was, but I did not have time to follow events clearly, as I felt my team instantly press closely around me, pushing me back into the factory. People were scattering, and as I looked over my shoulder across the yard I saw Lenin drop to the ground. Several men were running from his side towards a woman, who threw the gun at them and vanished into the crowd. Then I was inside, frustratingly unable to see any more.

"What's happening?" I demanded of my team.

At a signal from Nina, Sonja broke away and went back outside, returning a minute later. "Lenin is being taken to hospital in his car," she reported, "and the woman has been caught."

"Right, I want to get us all back to the Kremlin," Nina announced before I could speak again. The agents nodded, and Rada was sent out to find our cars and have the drivers bring them round to the yard.

* * *

Nina and Rada travelled with me in the first car, along with Sergei, one of my Department Thirteen agents for the evening; the rest of my escort followed in the second car. When we arrived at the Kremlin it was clear from activity around the palace building that Lenin had been taken to his suite, not to the hospital. There were cars clustered around the entrance, and lights glowing from almost all the windows. Aleksandra and I met at the barracks and went straight to her office, where I instructed Nina to take the girls and hang around the palace and send me regular reports on what was happening.

"I recognised the woman," Aleksandra told me when we were alone.

"The one who shot him?"

"Yes. Her name is Fanya Kaplan; she's a party member."

I was amazed. "Lenin shot by one of his own?" I couldn't help laughing. "I mean, I know the speech was boring, but surely it wasn't that bad!"

She looked surprised. "Didn't you find it inspiring?" she asked with a raised eyebrow.

As the new girl, I didn't want to seem critical of the people who had brought about the revolution, but adrenalin was flowing, and my honesty wouldn't allow me to hold back.

"I wanted to hear about Russia, what we are doing to put right all the injustices of the past, but instead he talks about world revolution. What use is that to us?"

She studied me before answering. "You and Fanya would get along well," she said carefully.

"Fanya Kaplan? Why?"

"She is very critical of Lenin's global ambitions for communism. I have spoken to her about it a few times, advised her to be more ... circumspect. You know that I am often outspoken about the way Comrade Ilyich runs things? Well she is even more vehement than I, and has already fallen foul of the leadership on several occasions." She peered intensely at me over he glasses. "Be careful, Nata, who you express your opinions to; in your position, it would not be good for you to be seen as too critical of the leaders."

I nodded. Holding my tongue was not one of my gifts, but I had to learn ~ my life depended on it.

Rada arrived at that moment, slightly out of breath after, presumably, running back with her news from the palace. "Lenin has locked himself in his suite," she reported. "Doctors have been brought in to treat him, and he is surrounded by guards."

"Is he badly hurt?" I asked.

"Two bullets hit him, but he's still alive."

"Why doesn't he go to the hospital?"

Rada shrugged. "Apparently he didn't feel safe going there, in case anyone else tries to kill him."

"I can see why," I said, grimly.

"It was an earlier attempt on his life that drove him to order the assassination of the ex-royals," Aleksandra informed me. "He thought that, while they lived, their supporters would keep trying to get them back on the throne."

"I'm beginning to understand how he feels. But the servants were no threat to him," I retorted. "He didn't need to have them killed."

She shook her head. "To be fair, I don't think he intended that to happen. It is more likely that Avadeyev exceeded his orders, to eradicate all witnesses."

"And I think it is Avadeyev who is the one who is now out to get me," I told her. "I am the only person still alive who knows what he did."

Aleksandra raised an eyebrow, but did not comment further.

After a little thought, I asked Rada to return to Nina and the team and bring them back to escort me home.

Chapter 19

~ *Wednesday 28th August 1918* ~

Dark cobbles under threatening skies. Although the first rays of the hidden sun were painting tendrils of pink, red and gold through the menacing, seething clouds that rose like a mountain range beyond the rooftops of Moscow, the light had yet to reach the courtyard where we assembled, which was a gloomy lake, awash in pools of black and grey. Distant thunder rumbled, like an altercation between irascible Norse gods (lacking only the surging Wagnerian music to complete the scene), as we emerged from beneath the towering cliff face of the garrison and clambered into our vehicles for the trip to the textile towns.

We had been working together on the details for nearly a month, Aleksandra and I, and now it was beginning at last. We would spend our first day together at Pavlovsky Posad, while she showed me what the factories were like and introduced me to the women who worked in them, then we would proceed to Orikavo, for more of the same. After that, I would strike out eastwards towards Nizhny, calling at Kovrov along the way, and she would continue to the towns north and west.

We shared a car for the short ride to the station, accompanied by a pair of our dark-suited security guards. Nervous and excited, I settled into the stiff leather seat, and watched as the rest of our escorts took up their positions in the three other vehicles. Drivers cranked the engines into life, then scrambled into position behind their steering wheels and our convoy set off, thundering through the arch and out into Red Square. There was a fresh breeze, though the expected rain had yet to arrive. The air was cool ~ summer was drawing to a close, and autumn was stalking the edges of the land, like a black bear, prowling, growling, waiting.

Our vehicles pulled up outside the pretentious front of Kursky station, with its columns and domes and arched windows, and our driver cut the engine and ran to open the door for us.

I looked around as I climbed out onto the pavement. Early morning passers-by had stopped to watch the sudden activity, curious at the arrival of so many people. It reminded me of that late-August morning, almost exactly a year earlier, when I had boarded the little train at Tzarskoye Selo with the royal retinue, bound for exile in Tobolsk. Their reign was already over by then, whereas the new royalty, Lenin, Stalin and the rest, were just getting their feet under the table.

A bright flash briefly lit the sky, and another drum-roll of thunder, closer now, sent a shiver through me as I recalled that day, and the events that followed it. I pushed the thought away. *'The past is past,'* I told myself, angrily. *'You were not responsible for it, and you cannot change what has happened.'* I knew it was the truth, but the memories would not let me rest.

We reached the booking hall just as the first heavy spots of rain began to beat against the pavements, and heads turned as we swept through like an invading army, accompanied by reverberating crashes of thunder like a salvo of cannon. What an entrance!

When we emerged onto the platform, the rain was pounding on the roof of the waiting train, pouring down upon us as we ran and quickly scrambled into the carriage which had been requisitioned for us in the name of the government. All along our route, trains had been reserved, hotel rooms commandeered, halls booked and factory owners placed on alert. I was fascinated at the way the Party machinery worked, like the locomotive at the front of our train, awesomely all-powerful, just as the Tsar had been. I found the comparison disconcerting.

* * *

Glaring flashes of lightning glittered on the streams of raindrops that raced diagonally across the windows of our carriage as we sliced through the bleak suburbs of Moscow and into the countryside, and the cracks of thunder, now overhead, were audible even above the constant clatter of the wheels on the track. Occasionally, I peered out at the smeared view of looming sky and wind-swept, tarnished-silver landscape, but mostly I watched my colleagues as they chatted. I was not inclined to join in; the act of holding my nerves under control left me with little strength for conversation.

It was mid-day by the time we reached Pavlovsky Posad, one of the grey, industrial towns that served the metropolis from a respectful distance. The storm, by then, had passed over, though rain still dripped from roofs and awnings, and thunder still bounced from sky to earth and back not far away.

An enthusiastic crowd greeted Aleksandra on the station platform. Local party officials jostled to welcome her, anxious to establish their credentials, to prove their loyalty to the cause. Their fawning embarrassed me, and looking at Aleksandra's face it appeared that she felt the same. However, there was business to be done, and we embarked on a programme of meetings and speeches that stretched into the night.

I enjoyed watching Aleksandra at work. She inspired people with her impassioned speeches, then chatted comfortably with them afterwards, answering questions, reassuring, comforting, urging them to keep supporting the new government. She introduced me to the party workers, and involved me in every discussion. I stood beside her on the improvised stages when she spoke to the men and women outside their factories, observed their tired faces, turned up to watch her, absorbing her words like a medicine ~ morphine, numbing the pain of their tedious, mechanical lives.

She told them about me, and I saw their initial surprise and suspicion as their eyes moved from her to inspect me, briefly. But we found that most people were willing to accept Aleksandra's endorsement of me, happy to learn that there was support for the cause, even from within the Tsar's own household; perhaps it helped them to feel a little less isolated.

We went into the cotton factories, and Aleksandra talked to the women working the looms, the engineers and the supervisors and the managers. She carefully showed me how the systems worked, and the things I should look for when I inspected the factories at Kovrov.

After a dizzying ~ almost frantic ~ round of appointments, we fell into our beds for a few hours sleep before rising again before dawn to move on to our next stop, Orekhovo, where the pattern was repeated. The mills seemed like dreadful places to me, but I discovered that they were vastly better than they had been before the revolution. Huge extractor fans were now in place, removing a good proportion of the choking fibres that floated in the air, and there were regulations and controls on the number of hours worked by the women in any one shift, as well as restrictions on the use of children.

By the time our two days together approached its end, I had the knowledge and confidence to begin addressing the last, small meeting myself, with her beside me for support. It was scary, yet exhilarating, and preparation for the role I was to play at Kovrov and Nizhny.

* * *

Another wet dawn, another convoy, another railway station. On the morning of the third day of our trip, Aleksandra and I parted company at Orekhovo. She would be heading north, to continue her whirlwind tour of factories and party offices, while I was going eastwards, with my own agenda.

On a platform opposite I saw Aleksandra's train arrive, and she waved to me as she climbed in with her retinue, the vanished from sight. I stood nervously, with my arms crossed, waiting for mine to arrive ~ the train to the industrial town of Kovrov, about two hundred miles from Moscow, where I had appointments with the workers and managers of the two principal factories. It was time to put my training into practice.

I felt a hand slip into the crook of my arm, and looked round to see Rada smiling reassuringly. "You'll be fine, don't worry," she said softly.

I gave her a rueful smile and shook my head. "This is not me, Rada, standing up in front of people, public speaking, committees, politics. All I want to do is to get to Nizhny and try to find out anything I can about Max's disappearance."

"It's only a day's delay," she said. "By this time tomorrow, we will be in Nizhny, and you can start poking around."

Sudden noise and bustling activity all around us heralded the arrival of our train, and my team closed in around me. Soon we were busy loading our baggage and scrambling aboard.

On the five hour journey I was alone with my whole security team for the first time since the trip began. They seemed to be getting along well enough, although the agents from Department Thirteen, Stanislav and Leo, spoke very little and revealed nothing. The four uniformed girls, however, were talkative and animated, chatting happily amongst themselves about everything from their families to the men they observed from the train window, and, just occasionally, about tactics and training. Even Sonja seemed more relaxed than at the start of the trip; perhaps she had just been nervous when it began.

I let them enjoy each other's company while I read through my notes and the itinerary of my visit.

Chapter 20

~ *Friday 30th August 1918* ~

Kovrov, a bleak industrial town, and a chill wind from the north nipped my cheeks as I stepped from the train. I was greeted by a delegation of representatives from the various cotton mills in and around the town, and even some local shopkeepers and tradesmen. Their spokesmen were not slow to express their disappointment that it was not Aleksandra herself arriving, but a mere assistant, someone they had never heard of before the posters arrived.

"I understand how you feel," I said, sensitive to their feelings and also rather nervous about the responsibility heaped on my shoulders. "Aleksandra will be here in November, but she wanted me to bring you news about the new employment laws that the government is passing, and to take back to her any messages you may wish to give me. I promise you, she will come. I am here to listen to you, to help if I can, and to report back on any problems."

They seemed to accept this, and led me to the vehicles they had organized to take me and my escort to the guesthouse where we were to stay overnight.

My luggage deposited, and Sonja left behind to keep an eye on things, I was whizzed off to the first of the public meetings they had arranged.

In what seemed like the blink of an eye, I was standing on the stage they had erected in the market square, before a small crowd of about thirty curious citizens, and reading out the message Aleksandra had given me to deliver. My nerves took control of my tongue, and I stammered my way through it, embarrassed at my poor delivery and conscious of their impatience. It took about five minutes, and by the time I had finished, the audience had melted away, like winter snow in the first rays of the sun.

Angry with myself, I apologised to the sturdy union leaders who had remained to the end. They laughed, putting me at ease, assuring me that the public rarely enjoyed listening to political speeches.

A short drive took us to a small workshop, where women sat at sewing machines, making traditional Russian garments. Magically, my nervousness disappeared; I felt comfortable with these people ~ ordinary citizens, working to survive, doing what generations had done before them. We chatted comfortably, and I read out Aleksandra's message again as they sat at their work-stations. This time I managed to do it with more assurance.

My next visit was one of two that had been worrying me since we planned the trip. With just my bodyguards, and the drivers provided by the local party, I arrived outside a big engineering plant on the outskirts of the town. The visit had been pre-arranged, and I was met by the owner, Valery Degtyarev and members of his board.

He led me inside, followed by his flunkies and flanked by my guards, and began to proudly show me the huge machines, pointing out the new ones. I noticed at once that the place was as silent as a church. "Why is there no production, Mr Degtyarev?" I asked.

"I sent all the employees home," he declared, "so that we can talk about the progress of our government contracts without all the din and bustle. It is a very noisy place."

I stopped walking, and he and his little entourage had to stop too, bumping into each other at the unexpected arrest of motion. I looked around the cavernous building, with its high, dirty roof and its oily machinery scattered like a child's building bricks discarded on the floor.

"I appreciate your thoughtfulness," I commented, dryly. "Are there no workers on the site at all?"

He shook his head. "Come to my office, and I will show you our production records; I am sure you will be impressed."

"Hmm," I said, distrustfully, meeting his eyes, and widening mine. "I'm sure I will."

'And how very convenient for you that I cannot speak to any of your employees,' I thought. He was willing to sacrifice several hours of lost production, just to prevent me talking to the workers ~ he must be hiding a great deal.

"As you know, Mr Degtyarev, I am here to represent the Council," I said as we stood in his office looking at a wall-chart displaying the progress of the various orders flowing through the factory. "They are concerned that several of your government contracts are behind schedule."

"It has become very difficult to get materials," he countered. "The steelworks are very slow in delivering what we need, and sometimes the quality is so poor that I have to send whole loads back to them."

That was reasonable. Many industries were suffering disruption by the White resistance, and I knew that steel production was one of them.

"Will you explain this chart for me please, Mr Degtyarev?"

"Why yes, of course," he effused.

He pointed to the lines of varying lengths that were drawn on it. "Each line represents an order, from the time it is received (here, for instance)" he pointed to one line, "... until completed and despatched. Each order is divided (as here, and here, for instance) according to the different stages of production."

"I see," I said thoughtfully. "And this chart?" I moved to

the one beside it.

"That is for planning machine utilisation," he explained. "Each machine can obviously only work on one job at a time, so we have to plan production to make best use of the equipment."

"So each line here represents one machine, and the numbers written above the line are the order numbers that correspond to those in the first chart?"

"Yes," he nodded, surprised that a woman had grasped the concept so quickly. He did not realise that Aleksandra had already briefed me on exactly this kind of thing.

"There are some lines without numbers," I commented, and pointed. "There is one, with what appears to be a name. What are they?"

He seemed to be taken by surprise at the question, and took a moment to search his mind for a convincing explanation, but recovered quickly. "They represent downtime. When a machine has to be taken out of production for servicing."

"I see," I said again. "There are so many of them, and some of the lines are rather long." I turned my head to study his face. "It must be inconvenient having machines out of production for such a long time. You must lose a lot of money."

He could not meet my eyes, and I knew that he was hiding something.

"Well," he said slowly, "the men can operate other machines, of course, but the loss of production is, as you say, inconvenient."

I had seen enough, and was deeply suspicious, but I was reluctant to start a confrontation that I did not feel equipped to handle, so I decided to end the meeting. "My sympathies, Mr Degtyarev," I said with a politeness that I did not feel. "Thank you for your time. I will tell Comrade

Kollontai what I have seen today. "

* * *

From the dingy engineering works, my hosts drove me to a park, where, beneath a statue of some civic grandee, I again delivered the message of encouragement from Aleksandra. A small crowd listened politely. I did not have her gift for oratory, but my confidence was growing, and they seemed pleased to hear what I had to say.

Afterwards, as I chatted with one or two union leaders, I saw a woman standing aside from the others. She was middle-aged, with a weathered face ~ not for her the pallid complexion of the factory workers, who were confined to gloomy interiors for all the daylight hours, she looked as though she was used to the outdoor life. She kept looking at me, as though she wished to speak, but seemed nervous to approach. When I looked again, a few minutes later, she was gone.

Next, I was driven to one of the textile mills. These, I had already discovered, were usually small places, dotted randomly around the towns where they had sprung up, most owned by the same family, usually with a manager appointed to each.

Union leaders met me and led me into the grey building ~ apparently, my visit did not warrant the attention of the manager. As we walked slowly from one, dust-covered, clanking machine to the next, I was able to speak to the workers, carefully writing down everything they wanted me to report back to Aleksandra. The air was thick with tiny fibres that floated like a fog, immediately irritating my airways and making me cough; the women who worked there told me that the extractor fans, installed by the factory owner on Aleksandra's insistence after her last visit, had lasted barely a year before breaking down, and

141

that workers were dying every day from respiratory problems. They also informed me that children were still employed there, but had been hidden from me by the factory managers, on orders from the owner.

It was time for me to flex my new muscles; I asked the union leader to take me to see the manager.

* * *

As I was admitted to the manager's office with my two bodyguards, he tried to dismiss Alma, the Shop Steward, but I insisted that she stay. He shrugged and waved a hand at two elegant chairs before his desk, a fine, mahogany piece with inlaid leather top. Leo and Stanislav took station beside the door, the three uniformed girls waited in the corridor.

Vasilyev, the manager, was plump, bald, and well-dressed; there was a smell of cigar smoke in the air. He tried to be effusive, but I could clearly see that he was nervous. Good. I would play on it.

But he pre-empted me, starting to speak before Alma and I were even seated in the chairs offered. "I hope you're not here to make trouble, Miss Tereshchenko. We are honest, hard-working people here, and I will not allow agitators to march in and stir up resentment."

"I'm glad you know who I am," I answered, quietly.

He nodded, his jowls flapping like the wattle of a chicken. "You are Natalie Tereshchenko, former maid to the Tsar, and now assistant to Aleksandra Kollontai. Am I supposed to be impressed?"

"Oh," I smiled, sweetly, "I am much more than that. I am comrade Kollontai's eyes and ears. While she is busy in one place, I am somewhere else ~ like a newsreel camera, travelling around, peering into corners, asking questions, reporting back." I paused and stared at him, letting my point sink home. But before he could answer, I added: "Tell me about the extractor fans, Mr Vasilyev."

"Now don't you try to blame me for those," he retorted, his voice becoming louder. "They are an example of the poor quality we have come to expect under this new government. I paid good money for them, and now they are useless!"

"That's interesting," I said, "because it is my understanding that you worked out a nice cut-price deal with your friend Mr Degtyarev, the owner of the engineering company just down the road."

He spluttered, his eyes becoming wide beneath his bushy black brows. "Who told you that?" he demanded.

"Do you think I would arrive here without first getting all the facts?" I said, my smile gone. "Why have they not been repaired?"

"There are not the skilled craftsmen to be found any more. Ask Degtyarev, he will tell you the same."

"I'm sure he will. How many of your workers have died so far this year?" I was deliberately jumping from one subject to another, to keep him off balance.

"What? How do you expect me to know that, off the top of my head?" He was becoming angrier with every word.

"If you cared, you would want to know, so that you could prevent it," I countered. I turned to Alma.

"Four hundred and thirteen," she said, answering the question of my eyes. "Sixty-five of them children."

"Children?" I repeated, returning my gaze to the manager.

He leapt to his feet, and I heard my escort behind me swing to readiness. "This interview is over!" he shouted. "Get out of my office at once!"

I stood up slowly. "I have seen and heard enough, Mr Vasilyev. I suggest that you start asking around among your friends for a job, because I will be recommending, on my return to the Kremlin, that this factory is placed in the hands of the workers, and you can tell that to your employers." I turned my back on him to leave.

"You will be sorry you crossed me!" I heard him shout to my back. "I have many friends!"

Leo opened the door for us, and smiled tensely as we sailed out.

"How did you know he did a deal with Degtyarev?" Alma asked as the door closed.

"I didn't," I said grimly, "but I'm beginning to understand people like him, and it seemed a fair guess."

Chapter 21

~ *Saturday 31st August 1918* ~

That night I slept poorly in the guest-house. Despite being tired from a busy schedule, my mind would not rest, flitting from events of the day to thoughts of Nizhny, and what I might find, and on, as always, to memories of my beloved Max. The bed was not particularly comfortable, but that was not what kept me awake, staring at the darkness. I was excited at the prospect of perhaps learning something that could lead me to Max, but also afraid that it would turn out to be fruitless.

Incredibly, it was still less than two months since we first met, yet so much had happened that it seemed longer. I smiled when I remembered how nervous he was when he introduced himself in the garden of the Ipatiev house in Yekaterinburg, and told me that he had been visited in a dream by an angel, Myriam ~ the same Myriam, my guardian angel, who had predicted to me, over a year earlier, that I would find love when I least expected it.

And I had fallen for Max at once; his soft, deep voice, his kindness and intelligence were just the start. He saved my life, plucking me from the death line in the middle of the night and leading me to his sister's café, where we made love for the first time.

As I stared into the darkness, I felt again the gentle touch of his hands and lips, and his soft, deep voice singing a Ukrainian folk song. Then we were on the run, fugitives from the gang who had murdered the royal family, led by Alexander Avadeyev and his brutal assistant, the Hungarian, Imre Nagy.

Perhaps I slipped into sleep, because I saw again the fight on the train, and heard the gunshot that wounded him and forced us to break our journey at Nizhny, to get medical help.

Where could he be? Had Avadeyev found him? I accepted that I may never find out, but I had to try; and if I could talk to the people who had helped us to slip out of Nizhny, perhaps they could give me some clues.

* * *

Bleary-eyed, I was up before sunrise, dressing for our early train. I would not be sorry to leave this dirty town and its corrupt businessmen behind. As I washed my face in the cold water from the jug on the wash-stand, I examined the scar on my forehead ~ healed, but still visible through the soft covering of my re-emerging hair. I would probably carry a mark for the rest of my life (whatever remained of it). Although I had been able to dispense with the bandages for several weeks, I chose to still wear one of my white, knitted hats at all times, so that I looked less like an escaped prisoner. Besides, I was wearing one in my photograph on the posters, so people would expect to see it.

Tensely, I looked around the room to ensure I had not forgotten anything, then snapped the clasps on my suitcase. Next stop Nizhny, and the start of my search for Max.

A knock on my door preceded the entry of Stanislav, who had been on overnight vigil outside my door. He effortlessly scooped up the suitcase, and together, we headed down the stairs, picking up Leo from his room as we passed. Outside, two cars were waiting. I waved cheerfully to the four soldiers waiting in one of them ~ Nina, Rada, Sonja and Marya ~ then climbed into the front vehicle with my two burly guards.

Fifteen minutes later we pulled up at the station entrance, just as the first glow of dawn was spreading across the sky. Stanislav, from the front passenger seat of the car, and Leo, from the back, beside me, jumped out, and stood like sentinels, one on each side of the door, their eyes alert, scanning the area left and right while they waited for me to alight. As I swung my legs out to follow, I saw the girls spilling from the vehicle behind, and running to take positions around me.

Then a strange thing happened. The last soldier, Sonja, was still running past me as my feet touched the ground, and I watched with surprise when she suddenly twisted as she ran, then stumbled and fell to the ground. At the same moment, I heard a crack, and all eyes turned briefly upwards towards the apparent source of the sound, the roof of a building opposite, where a small puff of grey smoke was drifting slowly upwards in the still air.

Leo grabbed me, pushing me towards the back of the car, shielding my body with his, while my soldiers dropped to their knees, their rifles pointing up towards the gunman's position. But I was slow, curious, watching over my shoulder as Leo tried to manoeuvre me to safety, and I saw another blossom of smoke appear briefly on the rooftop as a second shot was discharged. There was a metallic 'ping' beside me and a gouge appeared in the paint on the top of my car at the same moment as the sound of the shot reached my ears; I imagined that I felt a puff of warm air on my face as the bullet whizzed away with a sound like an angry bee.

Losing patience with me for dallying, Leo picked me up bodily and carried me around the car to the shelter of the far side, where he dumped me on the pavement, pushing my head down behind the protective metalwork. Stanislav joined us from the opposite end of the car, a pistol in his hand, peering over the roof.

By this time, people around us were becoming aware that something was happening, and there were some screams as they ran for the shelter of the station. I raised myself a little and looked up to the roof of the building again, in time to see a figure rise to its feet, briefly silhouetted against the skyline. There was a loud burst of rifle-fire from my army guard, and the figure collapsed.

The soldiers quickly confided, Nina and Rada ran towards the building, while Marya crouched beside Sonja, administering first aid to a bloody wound in her upper body. Stanislav turned and roughly shoved a way through the cowering crowd for Leo to lead me towards the station entrance.

* * *

We reached the big doors, and Leo tried to push me into the shelter of the building, but I squirmed free. "No, the danger is past," I insisted, shaking my head. "The sniper is down. Sonja is my priority now, I will not leave until she is taken care of."

Reluctantly, Leo left me with Stanislav and began talking to some of the people nearby, eventually dispatching someone who knew of a doctor practising close to the station. I turned suddenly and pushed through the crowd to the ticket desk ~ with Stanislav belatedly following ~ to instruct a clerk to telephone for an ambulance.

When it was done, he angrily told me off: "How can I do my job if you do not co-operate? You should have told me what you wanted to do." he hissed.

"I'm sorry," I said. "It was an impulse."

"You made me look like an amateur," he grumbled.

I could see his point, and apologised again. "I will try to

warn you next time."

"Next time?" he spluttered.

Fortunately, Leo returned and the three of us went outside again. We began persuading the crowd to disperse, telling them that the excitement was over, gently but determinedly moving them away from the little body lying in the road.

I made my way to where Marya was kneeling over Sonja. The girl appeared to be unconscious, a large red stain covering her tunic top, dripping onto the hard surface beneath her, and Marya was pressing a blood-soaked bundle of cloth against the wound to stem the flow. I crouched down beside them, putting my arm around Marya's shoulder, and she turned to me, a grim, sad expression on her face.

"That bullet was meant for you," she said. "Sonja saved your life without even knowing it."

I nodded. Sonja was unlucky to have intercepted the shot.

A man, clearly the doctor, arrived carrying a brown bag, bustling through the crowd of onlookers. I moved out of the way, and he began to examine Sonja.

While we waited, Nina and Rada returned from the building. Nina was shaking her head before I even asked.

"We found blood and cartridge cases on the roof, by the parapet, but no body and no weapon. The sniper has been removed ~ presumably he had associates."

Shortly, an ambulance arrived, and we watched as the crew consulted with the doctor. They gently lifted Sonja onto a stretcher and carried her to the back of the vehicle. I wanted to go with them to the hospital, but my team was adamant.

"You cannot," Leo stated. "There is nothing you can do, and you must continue the journey; people are expecting you."

Nina nodded her agreement. "Marya can accompany her, then rejoin us later."

Reluctantly, I agreed, and soon the two girls were on their way to the hospital.

* * *

Because of the delay we had missed the planned early train, but it was a frequent service and within half an hour our depleted group was in a carriage rattling its way to Nizhny.

"It had to be someone paid by Vasilyev, the mill manager," Leo declared as we sat in a huddle, discussing the incident. "I heard his threat as you left his office."

"Well, perhaps he is the most likely candidate for this attempt," Nina agreed, "but that doesn't explain the two previous attacks."

I looked at Leo and Stanislav as I added my own thought. "What about Stalin? He is unhappy about me being on the team, and Lenin warned me to beware of him."

Stalin, as head of Department Thirteen, was their boss. It was his personal creation, and though they had taken good care of me, I could not be certain of their loyalty to me if commanded otherwise. He and Stanislav had already saved my life once, and I was sure they had developed an affection for me, but I had to assume that they would follow orders, no matter what they entailed.

Leo was shaking his head. "I've not heard of any directive against you," he said.

I studied his face intently, trying to see through his apparent sincerity. "I suspect you would be the last to know, unless he wanted you to do the deed," I replied.

He shrugged. "I suppose so."

150

"Stalin didn't know about you at the time of the car incident," Rada added.

"True," I replied, nodding. "Anyway, my money is on the Whites. They can't be happy that I have changed sides."

"But why go to all this trouble? You are no threat to them," Nina said.

"Yes," I agreed, "but perhaps they would rather I was dead than working for the Communists."

We lapsed into silence, as each of us contemplated the possibilities.

Suddenly, an idea formed, and I blurted it out as it grew in my mind, before I had thought it through. "Maybe they weren't trying to kill me! Perhaps they want to capture me."

Rada, who had said nothing so far, laughed. "The man with the car was definitely out to take your life, and today's rifleman was not aiming for effect."

"Oh yes," I said, glumly. "Not much room for doubt, then. They want me dead, whoever they are."

Chapter 22

~ *Nizhny Novgorod* ~

I felt a surge of excitement as the train eased through the complex web of railway lines that converged on Nizhny Novgorod station. With small lurches and bumps, it jerked to a stop, and I cast a nervous look at Rada, before standing and following Stanislav through the carriage toward the doors.

The air was fresh as we spilled out onto the platform, and I took a deep breath to calm myself. Stanislav called a porter, who hurried over with a trolley for our baggage, then helped him to load it. I began to walk slowly towards the exit, my protectors forming into a square around me.

When we emerged into the concourse, we were met by a middle aged man with a large moustache, who smiled and reached out a hand. "Comrade Sister Tereshchenko, welcome," he said in a deep, almost theatrical voice. "Yakov asked me to be your host here. I am Alexei Maximovich Peshkov; I would like to invite you to stay at my house while you are in Nizhny."

I had been expecting to meet him; Aleksandra and Yakov both knew him well, and had told me about him in glowing terms. He was better known as Maxim Gorky, a famous author and activist for the communist cause. I saw a tall man, broad shouldered, with a friendly, intelligent, lined face.

"Maxim, hello," I said. "Yakov told me you would be here. I am sorry to arrive late, there was .. an incident in Kovrov that delayed our departure."

"Nothing serious, I hope?" He seemed genuinely

concerned, but I was already assessing him. Aspects of my true past were known to everyone in the party, and there had been three attempts on my life in as many weeks; I did not know who could really be trusted. I had already been wondering if Sverdlov had assigned Gorky to spy on me while I was in Nizhny.

"No," I replied, smiling reassuringly. "Nothing to worry about."

He blessed us with another broad, toothy grin. "Good."

We began walking towards the exit. "Now, we could take a taxi to my home ..." He paused, looking over his shoulder at my entourage and the porter with his stack of luggage rumbling along behind us. "Make that several taxis," he laughed. "Or we could walk across the square. It's not far."

I could not help liking him, he seemed so affable. "I am in your hands," I replied, returning his smile.

"Good," he said again. "Then let us enjoy a walk."

* * *

We emerged into the bright sunlight and paused beside the road, where he called a cab and instructed the driver to take our cases and bags to his address. Then we continued across the busy street ~ with horses, cars and trams all going about their various businesses ~ and on into the city centre. As we ambled along wide pavements, my host proudly pointed out the history and commerce at the city's bright, lively heart. Smaller than Moscow, Nizhny was nevertheless an impressive place. Shops were open ~ though many had little on display in their windows, I noticed ~ and a good number of people were out in the pleasant warmth of late summer.

After a short walk, we arrived at a busy market square. Nizhny had many mouths to feed, and although the economy still showed no signs of recovery after the war with Germany, the square was bustling with activity. Pens were jammed with noisy animals, auctioneers were bawling, stalls were selling everything from bread to blankets and cheese to chairs.

We chatted as we walked. I knew that Gorky had been a friend of Lenin for a while before the revolution, but was now a fierce critic. It wasn't long before he was telling me about their arguments. He laughed as he remembered once calling Lenin a tyrant in a newspaper article, for his brutal regime of arrests and murders.

"He tried to have me arrested," he grinned. Then his expression clouded. "Lenin and his associates are no better than the Tsar," he told me. "They consider it possible to commit all kinds of crimes in the name of the new regime, just because they can."

The admission surprised me, and his bravado. He did not know that I would not report straight back to Lenin. However, his words confirmed the opinion, first expressed to me by Sacha, and later reinforced in my own mind, that the new rulers were not the benign leaders they tried to portray.

* * *

We walked around the market, stopping sometimes at a stall to look at the goods for sale, my depleted squad nervously pressing tightly against me in the surging crowd, their eyes everywhere. Gorky spoke to nearly everyone we met ~ he seemed to be well known and liked by all.

At the centre of the square, a tall stone column rose, with a statue of a man in military uniform at the top, a sword in his hand, and mythical beasts spouting water into a great circular pool at its base.

I had paused to enjoy the sight and sound of the water

gushing and splashing, and the people happily sitting on the stone benches, chatting, when a man suddenly thrust himself out from the throng and lurched towards me. There was a look in his eyes that gave us a moment's warning, and my guards immediately stepped ahead of me to intercept him. But before they reached him, he pulled a hand from inside his ragged coat pocket, and pointed a pistol at me.

"Traitor!" he shouted before pulling the trigger. That insult saved my life. In the second that it took to utter those two syllables, Leo and Stanislav had grabbed his hand and spoilt his aim. The crack of the shot was accompanied by a sound like the ringing of a small bell, as the bullet ricocheted from the pavement between us and whistled through the air above my head like a wild spirit escaping from hell.

'Oh, not again!' I thought.

Instantly, the man was borne to the ground, and the gun wrested from his fingers. I quickly crossed the short distance to stand before him, and my men lifted him to his feet to face me. At last we had captured someone; perhaps now I could have some answers.

When he saw me close to him, he again shouted "Traitor!" his face contorted with hate.

"Why do you accuse me of that?" I asked.

His only reply was to spit at me.

I recoiled, wiping my face with my sleeve, then tried again. "What have I done to make you so angry?"

He subsided into a sullen silence, his head lowered; he looked defeated. He was only about eighteen, no older than me, with unruly brown hair and a straggly beard.

I turned to Leo and Stanislav. "Can you loosen your hold on him a little, please?" Their eyes widened with surprise, but they did as I had asked, their hands still around his arms, but loose enough to allow him to stand up straight. Suspiciously, the man raised his head and looked defiantly at me.

"Who paid you to do this?" I asked.

He glared at me for a moment, then began to laugh. "Paid?" he spluttered. "I do not need payment to kill a traitor!"

"Who have I betrayed?" I asked.

"You helped these animals to murder our beloved Tsar, and now you are enjoying your reward," he shouted defiantly.

So that was it. How easy it was to misunderstand, especially if it fitted the picture you wanted to see. I longed to tell him the truth, but it was clear that there could be no placating this man, no explanation that would satisfy him. I turned to Leo and Stanislav. "Please check that he has no more weapons, then release him."

They stared at me in amazement, each still holding one of the man's arms. Leo looked down at the ground before him, thoughtful, shaking his head, then raised his face to me, asking a silent question. Stanislav's gaze at me never wavered, his expression unreadable. Nevertheless, they checked his pockets and patted him down to be sure that he was not carrying anything, then took their hands away, as I requested. I could see, however, that they were ready to instantly grab him if he made any sudden movement.

I returned my attention to the man. "I want you to return to the people who sent you here," I said, stepping closer to him, "and tell them that I am not what you think, nor am I guilty of the crime for which they accuse me. However, also tell them that I resent people trying to kill me."

I paused, my face now close to his, staring into his wild, brown eyes. "Now," I continued, "I do not condone violence, but my life is important to me. If you, or anyone else, try to hurt me again, they will not be spared as I am sparing you this one time. I can promise you that these men who are beside you now can be as mean as a mother bear defending her cub, and your death will not be pleasant or quick. Do you understand?"

He did not move, his expression did not change as he returned my gaze.

I flicked my eyes to Leo and Stanislav, and raised an eyebrow. They each raised a beefy hand to grip the young man's arms between shoulder and elbow, visibly squeezing, their fingers digging into the flesh beneath his thin jacket. I saw his eyes bulge with sudden pain, and his mouth twisted as he fought the urge to cry out.

"I need to know that you are getting this message," I said, softly. "And you will not be released until you answer."

For a moment, he remained resolute. But I could see that his brain was working hard, weighing up his chances. Eventually he looked me in the eye and nodded, once, quickly.

"Are you sure about this?" Leo asked me.

"Yes," I replied. "We would gain nothing by holding him, and little from torturing him." I looked Leo square in the eyes as I said that, knowing as I did that Department Thirteen used methods that held human life in little regard. "Perhaps he will tell them that I am weak, but I will not have anyone tortured in my name."

With a shrug, Leo and Stanislav released the man's arms, and after a confused look at me, he scuttled off into the crowd.

Chapter 23

~ *Sunday 1st September 1918* ~

"This is a wild goose chase," grumbled Stanislav.

I couldn't argue, the odds against success were long. "Just humour me, please," I implored.

It was Sunday morning, and the six of us were spending our only rest day crammed into Gorky's car ~ fortunately a large one ~ driving around Nizhny, looking for a particular guest-house, the home of Yelena Novikov. It was our second day in the city, and we could have been enjoying some leisure time, but I could not wait another day. Five weeks earlier, my beloved Max and I had parted at that house, taking separate routes to flee the grasping clutches of a band of ruthless killers. Now I was hoping to return to it in search of clues to his disappearance.

I had described the location to Gorky, who was born and raised in Nizhny, and he was taking us from one place to another, hoping to find one that I recognised. Stanislav was right; it was a huge city, and the only thing I could say for sure was that the house was near the river.

But we were lucky, and after only a few tries I saw the little corner house. "That's it! But don't stop here," I instructed Gorky. "I don't want to frighten Yelena. Drop me off round the corner."

We cruised to a halt a street further on from the guest-house, and I climbed out. "Please stay out of sight. Watch from a distance, if you wish, but Yelena is a sweet and kind woman so you don't have to worry about me. Meet you back here in an hour?"

Gorky waved a hand in a casual salute, and the security

159

team muttered something that I took to be reluctant assent.

It was a strange experience, walking up the short path to Yelena's front door again. The pretty garden was blooming with bright, summer flowers, just as when I left, and the view across the the river was the same, except for the absence of the circus. I had not expected to return, but I felt a pleasurable excitement at the thought of seeing her again. Max and I had stayed there on our last night together, and Yelena had taken me from this garden to the convent, from where my journey to Moscow had begun.

I knocked, and waited. Nothing happened. After a while, I knocked again. There was not a sound from inside, yet I was sure she was there. I had a feeling that I was being observed.

I crouched down and pushed open the letterbox. "Yelena, it is Natalie. Are you home?" I called softly through the slot. I heard a little movement, and stood up, hoping she would open the door.

* * *

The door opened, and Yelena's face peered nervously out.

"I am here as your friend," I told her gently.

She smiled, a wan, sad smile, then held to door for me to enter.

We sat together in her little front drawing room, where we had met the men from the circus. Though she was pleased to see me, I could tell that she was changed; it was clear that something had happened in the short time since we had last met. She looked tired, and her eyes had a haunted look about them. I explained that I was now working for the government. It was important that she knew I was being completely open with her, and also that her secret was safe with me.

As she gradually began to relax, she told me some of the news. Much had happened in the weeks since I had left. Our friend Dmitri was no longer the chief of police, Avadeyev had replaced him with one of his own men. "The city belongs to Avadeyev, now; it is not a good place," she said. And, of course, behind Avadeyev lurked the politically ambitious figure of Yurovsky, close friend of Stalin. I felt a tightening inside ~ I was blithely blundering into the hungry bear's cave like a lost goat.

"Is Dmitri safe?" I asked.

"Yes, dear. He wisely moved out of Nizhny, with his wife and teenage daughter."

That was one piece of good news; Dmitri had been kind to Max and me. It was Dmitri who had introduced us to Yelena.

She told me that Vadim Ippolitov, the man who had organised Max's escape, had been murdered by Avadeyev. He was caught carrying copies of a newsletter for the White Underground, and, although there were no details of the members of the group, the messages were incriminating enough to seal his fate.

"And, Natalie," she said, leaning towards me to emphasis the seriousness of her words. "There is something you should know. The sheets Vadim was carrying said that there was a survivor of the assassination, a young woman, who had been smuggled to Moscow. Avadeyev now knows that you are alive, and where you are."

I nodded. "More than that, Yelena dear. I bumped into Yurovsky in Moscow, so I expect he has told Avadeyev about me, including the fact that I am in Nizhny."

"Why are you involved with them, Natalie?" she enquired. "I thought you would be absorbed into the White Underground, to help the fight to re-establish the monarchy."

"It's complicated," I told her. "For one thing, I don't want to be part of a new royal family. Even though I have misgivings about the new system, I still think people should choose their leaders, not be ruled from above. I set out to try to find myself a job, and wound up working as a secretary for the Party Secretary, Yakov Sverdlov, and the Women's Commissar, Aleksandra Kollontai. They didn't know who I was, until Yurovsky saw me and told them everything."

"And then ...?" she asked.

I smiled. "And then Aleksandra and Yakov stood by me, and persuaded the Council to let me work with them."

She shook her head in wonder.

I enquired about the little convent, and the nuns who had smuggled me out of the city. "It has been closed," she informed me, "as has the monastery in Makaryevo. But the nuns are unharmed; they have been dispersed to work in what few churches remain open. Nancy came by, and brought me your diaries and other possessions." She stood. "Wait a moment, I will get them for you."

I was overjoyed, something else to smile about; my diaries were safe. When Nancy helped to disguise me as a nun for my escape she had rightly insisted that I carried nothing that could link me to the girl who had worked for the Tsar and his family, and who was witness to their murder. I had been resigned to losing my diaries, which were a complete record of my life at Alexander Palace since I was old enough to hold a pencil, and were incriminating evidence of my past.

She returned, carrying a small bundle of clothes, and placed them in my hands; I could feel the exercise books, in which my diaries were written, wrapped between the layers of cloth, just as I had left them. I felt a surge of joy, and cradled them in my arms for a moment, a silly expression on my face. Not only was I glad to be reunited with my past, but it was also a relief to have them in my possession, to know that they had not fallen into the wrong hands.

* * *

But I had another matter to deal with, the reason for my visit. "Yelena," I said, putting the little pile on the table, "I have to find Max. The circus disappeared without delivering him to Moscow. I have no idea where he is or how to find him."

She looked puzzled. "How can something as big as a travelling circus just disappear?"

I shrugged. "My friends are looking for it, but the train was left in a siding at Kotelnich, and the circus didn't show up at Moscow or Petrograd where they were supposed to be performing."

"I don't know how we can find out any more," she said thoughtfully. "With Ippolitov dead, I have no link with them at all."

I was disappointed that this avenue of enquiry, upon which I had placed so much hope, had proved to be a cul-de-sac, but it would do no good to dwell on it. It was good to see Yelena again, and we chatted freely. For all that she appeared outwardly to live a relatively simple life, she was a deep, intelligent woman, as I had discovered when we first met. It was necessary to pay attention when she spoke, for there was often much hidden meaning in her words.

Though there was still sadness in her eyes, I felt that she seemed a little brighter by the time I had to leave. I would have liked to have stayed longer, but there was a meeting to be addressed, my biggest task yet as Aleksandra's envoy. So we hugged at her doorstep, and waved goodbye as I turned the corner, my bundle of secrets clutched tightly to my breast.

The late-August sky was pastel blue, dotted with wandering clouds, and the river off to my right glittered like diamonds in the early-afternoon sun. People, dressed in their Sunday best, were out walking; couples and small groups passed me, some smiling a greeting. I paused to take in the peaceful scene, a moment of normality in the upheaval of my life. I took a deep breath, savouring the heady smell of summer blossom.

Carriages passed me, with smartly liveried drivers seated high, leather reins trailing from their hands, their elegantly dressed passengers visible through the windows, and the horses tossing their beautifully beribboned heads and tails. On the opposite side of the road, travelling in the other direction (as though to emphasise the contrast between the old and the new) gleaming motor cars chugged along, leaving a trail of blue smoke that drifted in the warm air for a while before slowly floating away over the green like will-o'-the-wisp.

Eventually, with a sigh, I urged myself into motion, as though with a flick of my reins, and set off to find the car with my companions.

Chapter 24

~ *Public Speaking* ~

On Sunday afternoon, as my last public engagement on Aleksandra's behalf, I was to address a meeting of women workers from the factories around Nizhny, in the main hall of the Trade Fair.

We arrived in two motor cars at the front entrance, and for a moment after alighting, I stopped to admire the architecture while my guards formed around me. The hall was a beautiful building, grand, brightly-coloured and ostentatious ~ factors that would normally be enough to repel me, yet they were somehow blended in such a way that the structure still managed to please my eyes by its perfect proportions.

I would have liked to have spent longer admiring it, but a large, noisy crowd was gathered outside ~ a few cheering, but many booing and shouting abuse ~ and a group of women waited to greet me, so I had to get down to business. One of the women, shouting above the cacophony, introduced herself to me as Ludmila Belskya, the leader of the Nizhny Novgorod Women's Soviet. She seemed nervous of the hostile element of the crowd, and indicated that we should get indoors as soon as possible.

My entourage pressed through the throng in tight diamond formation, like a spearhead ~ Stanislav in front, Nina and Rada on each side of me, and Leo covering my rear. I followed Stanislav's big back, feeling very anxious, the girls pressing close to protect me, as the volume of the voices rose to a frightening din and the mob pushed and jostled with outstretched hands, trying to grab at me. I was carrying my precious package from Yelena in a shopping bag ~ I was determined not to part with my diaries again ~ and held onto it tightly, lest someone should snatch it.

Once inside, with the doors closed behind us, the dreadful noise was muffled, and the team reformed into a looser, square pattern ~ Leo walking ahead of Rada on one side of me, Nina ahead of Stanislav on the other. I could see that they were still very tense, their heads constantly turning, their eyes checking every shadow, every movement, their guns at the ready. We walked across a large, carpeted foyer to a corridor that brought us, shortly, to the hall itself, and we emerged onto a broad stage at one end of the huge hall. My heart jumped when I saw the size of the crowd I was to address. It is hard to describe the scale of the enormous room ~ high-ceilinged, as wide as a circus ring, and twice as long ~ and it was filled to capacity. It was the largest gathering I had yet attended, including those where Aleksandra was the speaker. A cheer rose from the women present as we appeared, but there were many more men in the crowd than I expected, and they, for the most part, remained silent.

I sat on a chair at the back of the stage, and my team took up positions beside me and in the wings. Ludmila Belskya opened the meeting and introduced the speakers who were to address the crowd ahead of me, one by one.

* * *

The first speaker, a local man, was greeted enthusiastically when he stepped up to the microphone. He spoke of Lenin and Stalin, praising the government for its actions on quelling the counter-revolution. It was high in rhetoric, and well received, though it sounded shallow to me, as though he was only saying the right things to stay on the winning side. Similarly with the man who followed.

I could see the shape the meeting was taking, and it was clear that I was the only woman speaker; this was not what I had been led to expect.

When I was called to speak, and rose from my chair to approach the front of the stage, the men in the crowd, previously attentive and enthusiastic, began to jeer and shout abuse. I stood at the microphone, looking down at the sea of hostile faces, feeling their hatred. There were some women, but they were outnumbered and shouted down by the men. It was clear from the things the men were were chanting that they felt that women had no place in politics, that our place was in the kitchen and in bed, and that we should accept servility to our masters.

Nervously, I opened the letter from Aleksandra, to read her message to the women, but my voice, even amplified, was drowned by the roar from the men. Angry, and close to tears, I turned to Ludmila Belskya. "How has this been allowed to happen?" I shouted.

She shrugged her shoulders, embarrassed. "I am sorry," she said, lamely.

I turned back to the microphone, unsure how to deal with a hostile crowd. My survival instincts were urging me to leave, but I had a responsibility to Aleksandra and the women of Nizhny. I cast my mind back, trying to think of something to help me break through the din. *'Well, they like Lenin,'* I thought.

"Vladimir Ilyich Lenin!" I shouted.

Enough of them heard the name to raise a cheer.

I followed up rapidly with: "Joseph Vissarionovich Stalin!" drawing a louder cheer, followed by a slight pause as they waited to hear the next name.

Taking advantage of the momentary lull, I added: "Aleksandra Mikhailovna Kollontai!" Raising my fist in the universal symbol of solidarity. They started another great yell, and a wave of fists appeared briefly above the crowd, until the men realised that they did not know the name, and their voices faded. But the women knew, and cheered loudly.

In the brief quiet that followed, I continued quickly:

"Those people built the revolution together, marching with the people, fighting alongside each other in the streets and in government. Lenin and Kollontai were both at the Winter Palace in 1905 when hundreds of men and women died on the instructions of the Empress. Lenin respects Kollontai. Will you insult him by rejecting her representative here today?"

Taking a chance, I paused, but they seemed prepared to listen to a little more. I began to read Aleksandra's message; there were a few jeers and catcalls, but on the whole they were more receptive than when I first came to the microphone. When I was finished, the women cheered me, while the men held a sullen silence.

I thanked them and waved. Then, still shaking, I glared at Ludmila Belskya as I snatched up my bag and coat from the chair on which I had been sitting, and left the stage, hastily joined by my escorts.

* * *

While not a total disaster, I was disappointed that the meeting had not achieved more, and I was glad it was the last one I would have to address on this trip. Public speaking was not my forté, and I hoped I would never have to do it again.

As we hurried out through the foyer, I saw a woman standing nervously to one side, looking intently at me. She was small in height, but strong in build, neatly, but unfashionably dressed; I thought I recognised her from somewhere. The way she gazed desperately at me made me break away from my escort and cross to join her.

I smiled and held out my hand. "Hello, I am Natalie Tereshchenko, did you want to speak to me?" Then I remembered where I had seen her before. "Weren't you in Kovrov on Friday?" I asked.

She reached out a small, brown, wrinkled hand to shake mine, nodding her head.

"Yes, I wanted to speak to you, but I lost my nerve; you seemed so busy, with so many important people around you. I hope you do not mind me coming today, Mistress," she said, shyly. "My name is Olgha Feldmann, you see." She stopped, looking flustered. "Oh, how can I explain? You will think I am crazy."

I shook my head. "I can see that you are not crazy, Olgha. What is it you want to tell me?"

She looked at her feet for a moment, then gathered herself and gazed into my eyes.

"A young man is staying with my husband and me. He has said that he knows you, and Stefan, my husband, sent me to speak to you." Her eyes peered out of a weather-beaten face and looked apprehensively into mine; she was as reluctant to be there as I had been in the hall, but, like me, her duty had overcome her discomfort.

"What is his name, this young man?" I asked, feeling a little lurch inside.

"Ah, well, there is part of the problem," she replied. "He has lost his memory, you see. We live outside Nizhny, beside the railway line; we have a small piece of land there. One morning, about a month ago, we found this man lying unconscious near the track. At first we thought he was dead, but he had a faint heartbeat, so we took him in and nursed him. He is about your age, a little older, perhaps, very tall and muscular, with light brown hair. We call him Ioann. Almost the only word he has been able to say is a name: 'Natalie, Natalie, Natalie.' When I came here to the market last week, I saw the poster about your visit, you see, and on a whim I took it home to show him, because of your name. He became excited when he saw your picture, pointing, and saying your name. So I have come back to find out if you are 'his' Natalie."

Could it be Max? The description fitted. My heart began to pound, and she must have seen how it affected me. "You know him?" she asked, hopefully.

I could hardly speak, hardly breathe! "Is he ... is he with you, here, today?" I finally managed to say.

She shook her head slowly. "No, he is still weak and confused, you see, and was unable to travel with me. He cannot remember what happened to him, but he had been badly beaten, and has a serious wound in his side."

Nervously I pointed to the place on my own side that corresponded to where Max was shot. "Here?" I said, simply, not daring to hope, yet feeling hope rising.

She nodded, quickly, a small smile pulling at her mouth. I, too, began to smile, though tears were also filling my eyes. Suddenly I felt a bond with her; we were two women who loved the same man, each in our way, and I had to hold her in my arms. We hugged, and could not hold back the tears, which flowed down my face.

"His name is Max," I told her, eventually, releasing her. "The wound was caused by a bullet, which was removed by a doctor in Nizhny. He is my..." My what? Lover? Uncle? (Our cover story when escaping from Yekaterinburg). No, I would be honest: "He is to be my husband. Do you have time to talk now? Shall we go somewhere quiet?"

Chapter 25

~ *Olgha* ~

We left the Trade Hall and found a little tea-shop nearby. Olgha and I sat alone in a quiet corner to chat, watched over from another table by Nina and Rada and the two Department Thirteen men. Outside, the warm late-afternoon passed slowly, people walking by were just visible as distorted shapes through the old glass of the windows.

Inside, we took time to get to know each other a little. Olgha and her husband Stefan owned a small farm to the west, where they grew wheat and potatoes and kept goats, pigs and chickens. They were childless, and when Max came into their lives, it was as though he had been sent from heaven for them to care for.

I could not help but see the contrast between Olgha and Sofiya, the ruthless, grasping woman who had claimed to be my mother. Though poor, just managing to survive from one harvest to the next, Olgha and her husband had room in their hearts to show love and compassion for another human being.

I told her about my past life as a Lady-in-Waiting in the Tsar's household, about our exile, and the murder of the royal family. As ever, I was reluctant to reveal my deepest secret, that of my royal connection.

As we talked, I saw that my security team, whose table was nearer the window than mine, were clearly concerned about something. After a consultation between the four of them, Nina and Rada suddenly left the café, and after a brief consultation with Leo, Stanislav came over to where I was sitting.

Looking nervously towards the window, he leaned close to me. "We must leave, now. Something is happening outside," he said, quietly.

"What?" I asked.

"I will explain later," he said, tensely. Suddenly, I felt fear grip me.

Quickly, I turned to Olgha. "May I come to see Max?" I asked.

"Of course. I am staying with my sister here tonight, then I will be travelling home early tomorrow. It is a slow journey, perhaps seven or eight hours in a cart over rough roads."

"Olgha," I said, breathlessly, "I would walk it if I had to. But for now I have to leave you. May I meet you here at dawn?"

She smiled and nodded.

* * *

Stanislav was clearly becoming agitated, glancing frequently at the door, so I stood to leave. As I kissed Olgha, he took my arm, again leaning close to whisper: "Quickly. We should go by the back door."

As if to emphasise his words, there was a sudden, short burst of gunfire outside. Whatever was happening must indeed be serious, I concluded, though I could not see anything.

With one man on each side of me, I was led to the counter. Leo spoke quickly with the woman there, who pointed to a door at the rear of the café. Within seconds, we were hurrying through the kitchens, past a startled cook, towards the back door. "What is happening?" I asked again.

Neither man spoke, but as we reached the back door

and Leo turned the handle to open it, he grabbed hold of my left arm, gripping it so firmly that I winced. At the same moment, Stanislav took my right, and I glared at them both, angry and puzzled.

"What ... ?" I began, as Leo stepped outside, dragging me behind him, with Stanislav following.

There, in the small courtyard behind the café, in the fading glow of the setting sun, stood a troop of soldiers, five men, with pistols drawn.

I turned my head to stare at Stanislav in amazement as he closed the café door, and he at least had the decency to appear abashed. When I looked back at Leo, he, too, was embarrassed, staring down at his shoes.

A man emerged from the group and took the two or three steps to reach us. I recognised him at once.

"Alexander Avadeyev!" I gasped.

He was grinning, but not the cynical, amused expression of Yurovsky, his boss, when he revealed my identity to Sverdlov ~ Avadeyev's smile was evil, the look of a man who expected sometime soon to remove a problem from his life. I felt a chill breeze blow over me in the red light of sunset.

"Did you think you could evade me forever?" he sneered. "Especially once your secret was out. And yet you are so stupid as to come here."

I glared at him, a quick retort forming in my mind. But I realised that anything I said would just help him, so, instead, I turned my head to face, first Stanislav, then Leo. "I thought you were my friends," I admonished.

"We have to obey orders," Leo said, quietly, unable to meet my eyes, but his grip on my arm relaxed a little, as though to show his shame.

"And so evil takes over the world," I replied, returning my gaze to Avadeyev.

His lips tightened. "Take her to the jail," he hissed, tilting his head in the direction of a motor van parked nearby. Leo and Stanislav gave me a little push, and we began to walk towards the van, followed by the other men. Avadeyev strode off in the direction of another vehicle that I recognised from my previous encounter with him as his own personal motor car.

When we reached the van, I was bundled in through the back doors, and sat on one of the wooden seats that were attached along the length of each side. Stanislav and Leo then departed, and I was joined by Avadayev's men, one sitting either side of me, while the other three took station opposite. No-one spoke as we began to move, swaying across the city. I did not feel inclined to say anything ~ I was too engrossed in trying to work out what my future might hold; it was not promising.

Eventually, the van stopped, and I was escorted into the back of the police station, which I recognised from the time Max and I had been there with Dmitri. Keys jangled and locks scraped as a door was opened and I was led down stairs and along a dingy corridor, illuminated by a single, bare electric light bulb hanging above our heads. There was a strong smell of body odour and urine, and I saw forlorn faces looking at me with subdued curiosity between iron bars as we walked past. More clattering of keys heralded the opening of an empty cell, and I was thrust inside.

* * *

As the door slammed behind me, and the men marched wordlessly away, I took account of my new home. Cold stone walls formed three sides, and the barred door marked the limit of the cell, perhaps seven feet long by five feet wide. There was no window, no furniture, not even a bed ~

a mattress leaned against one wall. That was it. There were no blankets, no washing facilities. A hole in the floor in one corner apparently served as a toilet, judging by its smell. These were the most basic of life's essentials.

I looked at the filthy mattress, unwilling to touch it, certain that it must be crawling with bugs, then I walked to the corridor end of the room and examined the barrier between me and freedom. It consisted of a row of vertical iron bars, cemented into the floor and ceiling, with strips crossing them at intervals; the gate set into it, by which I had been admitted, was of similar design, hanging on heavy hinges and with an enormous steel lock.

A slight movement in the half-light ahead caught my eye. I looked across at the bars of the cell opposite, and jumped when I realised that there was a man in the shadows behind them. A pale face, with staring eyes looked at me with dull curiosity. Shaken, uncomfortable under his scrutiny, I turned away and walked the four paces to the far end of the cell, where I stopped, obscured from his eyes by the darkness (I hoped), trying to think. What would happen to me now? Could I escape? How could I notify Aleksandra or Yakov?

Eventually, my legs and head aching, I lowered the mattress to the floor and gingerly sat on it. It seemed to be filled with straw. It felt damp, and smelled of mould ... and worse. After a while, the light in the corridor went out. Plunged into total darkness, there was nothing else to do but try to sleep. Wearily, I stretched out on the mattress, my skin itching at the thought of what might be sharing my bed with me.

Chapter 26

~ *Monday 2nd September 1918* ~

Later ~ I have no idea how much time has passed, cannot not even be sure if I have slept or not ~ I hear the sound of footsteps in the corridor and the grinding of keys in the lock. I open my eyes as a flashlight probes the darkness of my cell. It sweeps the tiny cave then hits my face, blinding me. Rough hands suddenly grab me, hauling me to my feet.

"What do you want?" I croak.

"Quiet!" hisses a male voice.

"I will not!" I reply loudly, suddenly angry.

In response I receive the back of a hand hard across my face, so hard that it spins my head, straining my neck and making my senses swim. Then I am pulled across the cell towards the door ~ pain raging in my cheek from the slap. I stumble and fall to my knees, but they do not slow, dragging me as I try to recover, my feet scraping on the concrete floor. As they haul me along the corridor, I hear surprised voices calling out from the neighbouring cells. My captors do not speak and do not stop until we reach the exit.

From the blackness of the jail, we suddenly emerge into the bright lights of the police station and stop. I blink in the glare as I regain my feet and look around me. I briefly see the faces of two strangers, then a bag is pulled down over my head from behind, and all becomes dark again. My hands are grabbed and pulled roughly behind me, where they are bound tightly with coarse rope or twine.

Then we begin walking again, their hands pushing at

the centre of my back, propelling me along. I feel cool, night air through my clothes ~ we are outside. After a few steps, perhaps ten yards, we stop again. I recognise the unmistakable smell of petrol and oil ~ a car of some sort. I hear a door open, then I am thrust forward, stumbling against the vehicle, cracking my shins on the unyielding metal with a stab of pain. Uncaring hands grab me from both sides and lift me off my feet, tossing me effortlessly through the air, head first. I gasp as I land on my back on the smooth floor of what I realise must be a van, perhaps the same van in which I arrived. I bounce and slide to a halt against something hard. Immediately, doors slam shut, close to my feet.

Then the engine roars into life and we are moving, the van swaying, rolling me from side to side uncontrollably.

* * *

The journey has lasted for perhaps half an hour. Occasionally I have heard male laughter and voices from the front of the vehicle, over the roar of the engine, and I wonder if they are watching me being rolled around, hitting my head and limbs on hard surfaces. I pull at the rope that bind my hands, trying to make some slack, but without success, and I am finding it hard to breathe inside the heavy cloth bag, with the fumes of the exhaust making me feel sick. It becomes even worse as we begin to lurch over unmade roads, and I am thrown helplessly into the air again and again, crashing back down on the steel floor.

At last we stop, but I cannot not feel any sense of relief, for I am sure that worse is to follow. I hear the doors open, letting in a wash of cool, clean air, then I feel hands grab each of my ankles. Effortlessly, they haul me feet first across the floor and out of the van, to crash onto the ground on my back. Now hands seize my arms and hoist me to my feet, then thrust me forward at a fast, stumbling walk. I know that my life counts as nothing to them, and I am sure that it will shortly be taken from me.

Then there is warmth and the sound of many voices around me, male voices raised in loud conversations, and there is the sickly smell of consumed alcohol. A cheer goes up. I am pulled through the crowd, hands grasping at my body as I pass, fondling my breasts, slapping my bottom, until suddenly we stop. The bag is brusquely lifted from my head, and I can see that I am in an agricultural shed of some kind, in the company of about thirty men, one of whom is Avadeyev. He is standing close, leering at me with an expression that combines hatred with triumph.

Wordlessly, while two of his men hold me by the arms, he raises both his hands and grips the edges of my dress at the top ~ where it buttons down the front ~ and jerks the two sides apart. The buttons pop and fly, revealing my white cotton blouse underneath.

Shivering with fear, I glare angrily at him. "You will regret this when Sverdlov hears about it," I rasp.

He laughs. "Sverdlov? How will he find out? And what would he care if he did? It was Sverdlov who signed the execution warrant on your precious royal family. He wants you dead almost as much as I do!"

The revelation stuns me. Sverdlov? Responsible for the murder of my friends? He must be lying; but why would he bother, when I am already his captive? I am shocked speechless, an empty feeling suddenly in my heart.

Before I can gather my wits, he is leaning closer, grinning like a lizard. I feel the heat of his breath on my face, smell the stink of his foul breath, can read the intent in his eyes as he rips my blouse open in the same way as he just disposed of my dress.

There are mutters of approval from around the room as

my chest is exposed, my small breasts unprotected by a brassiere. He turns briefly away from me to grin at his cohorts. Then his hands are suddenly at my shoulders, yanking the remains of my upper garments down my arms and body. They fall to the floor at my feet, and I am exposed, naked to the waist, wearing nothing but my knickers and a petticoat.

I fight back the tears, unable to cover myself, seeing where this is going, refusing to beg this despicable animal for mercy. Instead I glare at him, staring into his eyes with all the disgust I feel for him.

He laughs again at me. Then, without warning, strikes me across the face with the back of his hand, for no other reason than the pleasure it gives him to abuse me while I am helpless. I cry out involuntarily, tasting blood in my mouth. He wastes no more time, reaching down to rip away my remaining clothes, leaving me completely naked before this roomful of men.

Ashamed and terrified, I close my eyes, the tears now flowing uncontrollably. They clearly plan to have their pleasure on my helpless body before, no doubt, killing me ~ and Avadeyev is to be the first.

"Turn her round," he instructs the men holding me. They obey, and then they push my head down so that I am doubled over, my most private parts revealed to all. As I feel his groin press against my buttocks, I remember that this was what happened to Polya when we were held captive with the royal family in Tobolsk. Like her, I try to press my legs together, to deny him access, but it does not stop him. Something is pressing close against my vagina, what it is I do not know for sure, but I feel it began to force its way inside me.

"Please, no!" I scream, and hear them all laugh. They begin to chant: "Fuck to death! Fuck to death!" Avadeyev's hands are gripping my hips, his fingers digging into my flesh, pulling himself into me.

I feel my senses swimming as my mind tries to shut out the nightmare, but I am jolted back into consciousness by a loud explosion from somewhere in the room behind me. The chanting stops, as though a radio has been turned off. Another five bangs follow in quick succession. Something warm splashes on my back, and all the hands holding me become slack and fall away. Released, I stand and turn to see what has happened. Avadeyev is lying on the floor at my feet, blood quickly forming a pool beneath him, as are the two men who had been holding me down.

I look around the hut, searching for an explanation. Standing at the far end, in the open doorway, with a cloud of cordite smoke rising slowly above her head, stands my saviour, Rada, with a heavy pistol in each hand. The remaining men cower before her, their hands in the air. They seem to have lost interest in me.

Chapter 27

~ *Rada* ~

I quickly pull up my clothes from around my ankles and try to arrange them around me, covering my nakedness. Then, as I secure the front of my dress with the few buttons that remain, I run through the crowd, which parts miraculously, like the Red Sea, to stand beside Rada.

When I arrive, she hands me a pistol. "I don't know how to use these things," I whisper.

"Don't worry about using it, just wave it around as though you do," she hisses.

I comply, seeing the terrified expressions on the faces of the men as they see it in my shaking hands pointing at them.

"What now?" I ask.

"You get outside first," she replies with a twist of her head towards the door behind us.

I slip past her, out into the cool night air. As I do so, I see her remove something from her belt, a kind of stick thing with a cylinder attached. There is a dull thud as she tosses it into the crowd, then she backs quickly outside and slams the door behind her.

"Run!" she bellows, demonstrating by her own action

I follow, holding up my long skirt. After about eight stumbling steps on the rough ground, the silence of the night is ripped by an enormous explosion behind us, and the area is lit up briefly as though by a searchlight. Rada throws herself to the ground, and I copy her. A blast of hot air sweeps past and over us, followed by pieces of corrugated iron and other debris that begin to rain down around us, the largest, fortunately, missing us.

When the shower stops, we pick ourselves up and stare at the shattered, smoking remains of the hut. There is not much left. A crater, about ten feet across, with a few beams still standing like gravestones around its perimeter to show where it had been, while the wreckage of the remainder is scattered in a large circle around us. Among that debris are things that looked disturbingly like twisted human bodies, or parts of them.

"Quite a bang," I comment. My terror of minutes ago has been replaced by a strange kind of calm, though my heart is still pounding in my chest.

"Hand grenade," she replies casually, shrugging.

"Impressive," I add.

"Yes," she says.

"Messy, too."

"Yes," she says again.

I look around. The sky is lightening, with only one or two of the brightest stars still visible, and the horizon off to our right is already yellow-grey, split with a slash of red cloud above the silhouetted rooftops of the city, promising that dawn is imminent. Northwards, beyond the smoking ruins of the shed, the ground rises to an embankment, a black shadow against the near-black of the sky beyond. As though on cue, with a whistle and a plume of orange-tinted smoke, dotted with a shower of sparks, the dark shape of a train clatters swiftly and noisily by along the top of the embankment, disappearing away to our left. Within a minute, it is gone, leaving only a trail of sooty, grey smoke that slowly drifts upwards and spreads into a translucent cloud.

There are no more buildings nearby; we are standing in open farmland, with just a clump of trees not far away to our right, and a line of poplars stretching east-to-west behind us, which I assume must have been beside the road by which I was delivered. I find that I am beginning to shiver.

"Are you ok?" Rada asked.

I nod, trying to avoid looking into the part of my mind that holds the recent events in the hut ~ the images in there are the stuff of nightmares.

"How did you find me?" I ask, curious, and anxious to start a fresh train of thought.

"I've been following you ever since you left the café."

"I've been puzzling about that. What exactly happened there?"

"Well," she says, arranging her thoughts in order. "From where we were sitting, near the window, I could see a group of soldiers hanging around outside. I thought there was something odd about the way they were loitering, so I told Stanislav and Leo. They tried to say it was not important, but Nina and I went out to investigate anyway. Even though we were in uniform, the men pointed guns at us and tried to arrest us. We resisted, and a fight broke out. Although they were waving their guns around, I think they were reluctant to use them against us in a busy shopping area, but one went off in the struggle anyway. The shot hit Nina, and she fell, but I managed to escape into the crowd of onlookers. The soldiers dared not fire their guns at me with so many people around, and though a couple of them pursued me, I was able to lose them."

"Nina? Oh no! How is she?"

"I don't know for sure; she didn't look good. I needed to get back to you, to warn you, so I had to leave her."

She pauses, the memory of abandoning her colleague troubling her, then shakes her head, as though to clear it, and continues:

"The trouble was, whichever way I approached the café,

there were soldiers blocking all access. By the time I had worked my way round to the back entrance, I saw them putting you in a van. I stole a bicycle and followed you to the police station. As soon as it got dark, I started to break in. But then they brought you out, so I followed again."

"On a bicycle?" I ask, incredulously.

She grins ~ I love that grin.

"No, I stole a police car." She points to a vehicle parked a short way off. Sure enough, it has the word 'Militsiya' painted on the side.

I find myself hugging her, words failing me, and then I realise that I am still holding the pistol she gave me in the hut.

"What if this thing had gone off?" I exclaim, suddenly realising the danger. "I could have killed someone!"

She looks at me quizzically, and I realise what a stupid thing I just said. Killing, after all, is what guns are designed for, and the people before whom I had been nervously waving that particular weapon had previously been clamouring for my own death.

"Anyway, it's empty," she informs me, taking it from my shaking hand and stuffing it into the wide belt of her uniform. "I emptied it into that bastard Avadeyev, and the men holding you."

Again I had to divert my mind from the images that suddenly filled it. "Do you always walk around with two pistols?" I ask.

She laughs. "No, only one as a rule. I took the other from the man who was supposed to be keeping guard outside the shed. Those men were not real soldiers, just a militia of local thugs, getting a thrill from the position of power. He was too interested in peering through the window at what was going on inside to notice me, and the rest of them were making so much noise that he didn't hear me creep up behind him with a knife in my hand."

I rub my swollen cheeks with the palm of my hand. Now that the pace of events has slowed, I am aware again of the pain in both of them, and the rawness inside my mouth from Avadeyev's last blow. I find that I can smile wryly at that thought ~ it was literally his last. I can relax, knowing that the brute is dead and can never harm me again.

We stand in silence for a while, looking at the ruins of the hut as I begin to fumble with my clothes, trying to re-arrange them a little better.

"Whoever owned that isn't going to be pleased when they find it like this," I comment, nodding towards the still-smoking foundations of the hut.

"We had better make good our escape then, before we're caught red-handed," Rada agrees. "We need to move on, at any rate. Where shall we go?"

"To find Max, of course!" I say decisively. "He is closer now than at any time since he walked away to join the circus.

"Which way?"

I point westwards. "Follow the railway line and check every farm until we find him."

Chapter 28

~ *An Arsenal* ~

Before leaving the scene of devastation, we have ransacked the van in which I was delivered. We found a bottle of vodka and some tobacco, which we have left, and a rifle, another pistol ~ in the holster of a brown leather belt ~ and several cartons of cartridges, all of which we have decided to liberate. The police car yielded nothing useful.

We have decided to leave the vehicles and walk, not wishing to be caught with evidence to connect us to what had happened here.

Rada hitches the rifle by its strap onto her back, then removes the purloined pistol from its holster, opens a flap in the handle, and extracts a kind of cage, containing bullets. She pulls back the top of the gun, and a bullet pops out and falls to the ground. Then she holds out the pistol to me.

I stare at her.

"Take it," she insists. "It's not loaded.'

To prove her point, she raises it above her head, pointing it at the sky, and clicks the triger a couple of times, before taking hold of the barrel and holding it out to me again.

Nervously, I comply, wrapping my hand gingerly around the hand-grip, keeping my fingers well away from the trigger, even though I know the gun is empty. It is big in my hands, which do not even completely circle the rectangular handle, and it is so heavy and unbalanced that it feels as though it wants to twist out of my grasp.

"Good," she says. "Always be careful how you handle it, and it will be your friend. Now, this," she points to a small lever, "is the safety catch. When it is this way, the gun cannot be fired. Keep it like that at all times until you need to use it."

I nod.

"If you ever need to fire it," she continued, "hold it with both hands, like this." She demonstrated with her own gun, holding it straight-armed, level with her eyes, pointing it out over the open fields.

I copy her, the gun drooping in my ineffectual grip.

"Tighter! Grip it firmly," she instructs.

I grasp it harder.

"Good," she says again. "Now, when it goes off, it will kick back." She mimicks the action by jerking the gun in my hands. "Using two hands will steady it a bit, but you have to be prepared for a jolt in your arms. It is a beast! Okay?"

"You're not expecting me to use this thing, are you?" I ask, seeing where she was leading.

She nods, tight-lipped.

"I hope not. But the way things have been going, I think you have to be ready to do just that. Now, it's not loaded, remember, but I want you to know what it is like to fire the gun, so let off the safety catch, put a finger on the trigger and pull."

The safety catch is right by my thumb, and easy to slide along. But when I hold the gun out at arm's length, as instructed, I find it quite hard to pull the trigger, and I add a finger from my left hand to help my right. As I pull it, I can see a small part at the back, just above my hands, slowly tilting. Eventually, the trigger gives, and the moving thing snicks back to where it started. When I release the trigger, there is a metallic click from inside the gun, which I also feel in the handle.

"Do it again," Rada orders.

I obey, and find it easier this time.

"Now three quick shots," she says.

"My arms are getting tired," I moan.

With an exaggerated exasperated expression, and a hand on her hip, she glares at me. "Just do it, Nata," she barks.

Chagrined, I obey.

She grins. "Well done. Now, if you have to shoot someone, aim here, if you can," she points at her chest. "It's the biggest target. The gun will jump as you fire it, and aiming at the biggest target means you stand a chance of hitting something."

She stops speaking for a moment while she fiddles with the cage she had removed from the handle of my gun, pressing all the bullets out with her fingers. When it is empty, she hands it to me. "That is the magazine," she says. "I want you to put bullets in it, one at a time."

As I take it from her, she holds out her other hand in which lay the bullets she has just removed, like a nest of lethal eggs.

"Take one, and lay it in the guide," she instructs.

After fumbling with my gun for a moment, I eventually tuck it under my armpit while I proceeded to do as she told me.

"Yes, that's it," she nods. "Press it in. Good. Now the next."

When it is full, she has me insert the magazine into the handle of the pistol and lock it in place.

"Aim at the trees."

"You're going to make me fire it, aren't you?"

She nods, then puts a hand on my arm. "Nata, it's just the two of us now. I need to know that you can protect yourself if … if I can't."

I am about to reply, but she presses on, raising her voice to over-ride me.

"Point the damn thing at the trees, will you!"

Obediently, I raise it and aim at the copse.

"Lock your elbows," she instructs. "Be ready for the kick. Look along the barrel at your target and squeeze the trigger smoothly."

I begin to pull the trigger, tense in the expectation of the explosion waiting to happen. There is a loud crack, which echoes briefly, and my arms feel as though I have run into a wall with them outstretched; a flock of birds rises in panic from the thicket.

"Now you are ready to face the world," Rada says grimly, taking the gun from my shaking fingers, setting the safety, and putting it into the holster we took with it from the van. She passes it to me, and I loop the belt over my head so that it drapes from one shoulder across my chest, like a sash.

"I hope I never have to use it," I confess.

"Having seen you in action, so do I," she grumbles.

Chapter 29

~ *Max* ~

After following a track that ran roughly south for a little way, we have now joined another, broader trail ~ the avenue of poplars I observed from the shack ~ heading west, parallel with the railway line. We are walking in silence, picking our way over the ruts and puddles, the rising sun behind us, casting our shadows long ahead, like a pair of fingers pointing the way. I realise that my shoes are inadequate. My head is reeling from the events of the last twenty-four hours, and various parts of my face and limbs are throbbing from the punishment they have suffered since I left the café.

Though I try to shut out the memories of what has happened in that shed, I might as well be trying to stop the sun from rising or the Volga from flowing out into the sea. And, over all the shame and fear, I keep hearing Avadeyev's voice telling me that Sverdlov, the same Yakov Sverdlov that took me to the ballet and kissed me tenderly at my door, was the man who ordered the deaths of the royal family and all the servants, and then had the nerve to be angry at me for not telling him about my past.

After a couple of hours, as the sun climbs and our shadows shorten, we begin to hear the heavy breathing of a horse behind us, accompanied by the creaking of its harness. We turn, and see a farm wagon pulled by a single old horse, and driven by a small woman.

"Olgha!" I exclaim, amazed that in this wilderness our paths have met.

She stops the cart, looking with surprise at us. "Natalie,

it's you! You looked like two bandits!"

Despite my mood, her words make me smile; a painful action. I realise that we must look quite a sight with all our guns, and the belts ~ decorated with rows of bullets ~ that were draped over our shoulders.

"What are you doing out here?" she continues. "I was disappointed when you didn't show up this morning, but assumed you had to be somewhere else."

"It's complicated," I say. "I'll explain later. This is my oldest and dearest friend, Radochka. Can we ride with you?"

"Of course," she smiles, sliding across the wooden bench seat to make room for us. "Jump up."

The board is just long enough for all three of us, and as soon as we have settled onto it she gives the reins a shake and the old horse begins to walk again.

As we sway slowly along, I tell her about my kidnap, and Rada's dramatic rescue. I cannot bring myself to recount the more sordid details, still trying as I am to put up a barrier in my mind to hide them away, to pretend they never happened.

"Look on the floor of the wagon, behind you," Olgha says suddenly, smiling.

I twist in my seat, and there lies the bag in which I was carrying my diaries when I first met her. I grin and hug her.

"In my haste to leave, under pressure from Leo and Stanislav, I forgot it," I say, lamely. "And thank goodness I did, because in there are all the secrets of my past life. They would surely have fallen into Avadeyev's hands."

"Yes, and that would have made your situation much worse," Rada mutters.

Absent-mindedly, I hum and nod, my thoughts still turned inwards, but then I am jolted out of them by the digging of an elbow into my ribs. Puzzled, I turn to look at

Rada, who has a strange expression on her face.

"What?" I ask.

She starts laughing. "Nata, how could it have been any worse than it was, silly?"

"Humph!" I grunt. "Sometimes I have serious doubts about your sense of humour."

But I see at last what she means, and have to suppress a grin.

* * *

The road wanders between fields defined by hedges and trees, sometimes taking a diversion around a wood, or a body of water. It is a fine, dry day ~ warm in the sun, but comfortable ~ and I feel my mood improving. The thought of finally seeing Max sends frequent little shivers of anticipation through me. We pass a few farms along the way, isolated little settlements, country people making the best they can of a hard existence. Smoke rises from the chimneys of some, and there are clusters of goats and cows in fenced pastures, but we see no people. I wonder if they are watching us pass from their windows, curious but wary.

The sun passes over our heads, and begins to disappear into a rolling bank of clouds that we have watched growing from the horizon in front of us.

At length, we pull off the road into an enclosure of wooden buildings ~ Olgha's and Stefan's farm.

It is bigger than I have been expecting. A white-painted, square-fronted house stands at the far end of the yard we have entered, with barns and animal pens ranged along either side of us, and the entrance now behind us open to the road.

A pig peers curiously over the top of a half-door in one low shed, and I can hear the bleating of a goat from within another.

A door opens in the house, and a black-and-white dog runs out to greet us, followed by two men. My heart suddenly begins to pound as though it will explode when I see them. One of them, the older of the two, and conspicuously the shorter, is presumably Stefan, Olgha's husband, but my eyes lock onto the other man. There is no longer any doubt, no mistaking the wild, blonde hair and broad shoulders. It is Max ~ I have found him at last!

As soon as the cart has stopped beside a stable, I leap from it onto the cobbled yard, stumbling as I land. I regain my balance and run towards Max, the dog barking at my feet. I see his face as he recognises me, and a big grin opens on it, though I notice in the process that he had lost some teeth.

"Natalie," he lisps, as though saying a prayer, his hands reaching for me. "Natalie, Natalie."

We clasp each other close, and I inhale his smell, feel his breath in my hair, his hands stroking my back.

"I thought I would never see you again," I sob.

In my peripheral vision I see Stefan cross the yard to begin releasing the horse from its shafts. Rada helps him, and I notice that they are in conversation, while Olgha comes to stand beside me.

"Olgha," I blurt at last, "this is Max. This is my Max. I was afraid they had killed him."

"They tried," she says softly, "and nearly succeeded. Come indoors, let's have something to eat and drink."

* * *

Max and I cling together as we follow Olgha into her kitchen, a large, open room that occupies the whole ground floor of the farmhouse, with a big scrubbed wooden table at one end, set with chairs, and a huge log-burning cooking stove at the other. Olgha makes a pot of strong tea, and sets it on the table. I pour a little for each of us into the pretty little cups she has brought from the dresser that almost fills the back wall. For Max and me, I add hot water and a spoonful of the jam that Olgha has placed in the centre of the table.

Rada and Stefan come in from the yard ~ they seem to be getting along well. Rada has taken off her brown army jacket while outside, and rolled up the sleeves of her shirt. She drapes the tunic over the back of a chair and, after looking to Stefan for approval, and receiving it with a nod, props her rifle against the dresser.

Stefan is lean and muscular, much shorter than Max, not much bigger than Olgha, in fact. He is dour, his leathery face seemingly unable to smile, his little eyes almost invisible in the mass of wrinkles, yet I feel a warmth in him ~ he cares, but shows it only in his ways, while hiding behind a serious expression. He had removed his hat as he entered the kitchen, hanging it on a hook beside the door, and his long, grey-brown hair is tied back in a pony-tail.

We sit together round the table, eating some bread and cheese and cake, while sipping our tea and getting to know each other.

While we chat, the kitchen becomes darker as, outside, the heavy clouds have arrived and rain has begun to fall. driven against the windows by sudden wild gusts of wind Olgha lights an oil lamp and hangs it on a hook that descends from the ceiling above the table, and we sit in its circle of light. It feels ... intimate, warm, as though we are a family.

I learn that Stefan inherited the farm from his parents, who died within only a few years of his marriage to Olgha, that Stefan is a blacksmith, and still keeps a forge and workshop, and that they have no children. Without family to help with the farm, they have struggled each year to get the crops in before winter, but they are blessed with good neighbours, who pitch in and help when they can. Stefan repays them by repairing machinery, shoeing their horses and sharpening knives.

Stefan asks to know more about Max and me, and I repeat what I have told Olgha about my life as a servant in the royal house, and subsequent escape from their murder. I also tell them both what I know of Max's past.

And all the time we are talking, Max and I are holding onto each other, as though to make sure we couldn't slip apart again. He has changed, physically and mentally. I discover that the beating he received from the circus gang broke two of his ribs, one arm and a cheekbone, as well as opening up his bullet wound again. I can see that he finds it hard to stand up as straight as before, and he walks slowly and carefully, as though each movement causes him pain. His mind wanders, too, and he does not speak, though he sometimes nods or shakes his head if necessary. Nevertheless, his hand grips mine, and he smiles his gappy smile every time I look at him.

Chapter 30

~ *Attack* ~

Our simple tea done, Stefan leans back and lights a pipe, and begins chatting easily with Rada. Olgha and I start clearing the table and washing the cups and plates; I feel relaxed and happy, despite all the terrible things that have happened. I am with my Max, and again I recall Myriam's words, when she visited me in the night nearly two years ago and promised that I would find love, and the home and family I have yearned for all my life. As I look fondly at Olgha, and at Stefan and Rada as they relax together, I know that this is the closest I have ever been to fulfilling that dream.

Suddenly the dog, which they call Malchik, and which has been asleep in his basket, raises his head with a grunt, then runs to the door, barking. Looking apprehensively at each other, Rada and I cross to the big window, and peer out. We are just in time to see a man run diagonally across the rain-lashed yard towards the pig-pen, doubled over, like a hunchback. He flattens himself into the recess of the pen door.

Another stands, half-hidden, behind the stable, a rifle clearly visible in his hands, and I see him raise it to his shoulder. As I shout a warning to Rada, the window panes suddenly shatter inwards, and a bullet slams into the far wall of the kitchen.

"Turn out the light," Rada calls over her shoulder to Olgha, pulling her pistol from her belt. She takes careful aim and fires a single shot through the broken window.

My pistol belt is lying on the sideboard that divides the

room, where I put it when I arrived. I run across and grab it as the room fades into darkness.

"How can Avadeyev's men have found me again so quickly?" I ask as I rejoin Rada, removing the gun from its holster and gazing out into the yard.

"Perhaps there were more of them than we realised," she shrugs, squinting along the barrel of her pistol and letting off another round.

"I have seen four men so far," Stefan says, looking out through a smaller window at the end of the kitchen. "Ioann … Max, take Olgha upstairs."

He reaches up and takes down a shotgun mounted on the wall, and quickly loads it from a box of cartridges. Then, slowly, he opens the window and rests the barrel of the gun on the sill, peering carefully out, scanning the yard for movement.

"If they are at the front, they must also be at the back!" Rada says suddenly. "Stefan, is there another door?"

He shakes his head. "No, at the back there is only the log store."

"Nata, take your gun and go upstairs with them," Rada orders me, nodding towards the staircase where Max and Olgha have begun to slowly climb. "Look out of the back windows, and shoot anything that moves! Oh, pass me my rifle before you go."

I nod, grabbing the rifle from beside the dresser and handing it to her. Then I run up the stairs, overhauling Olgha and Max halfway. I slip past them and continue to the top, then pause to look around.

There is a little light entering via a small landing window to my left, and by it I can see a short hallway, with four doors off, all open. I turn right, towards the back of the house, and run to the door of the left-hand room.

The sight that greets me is almost surreal. In that pretty,

half-dark room, with a floral bedspread and neat furniture, I see the bulk of a man in a dripping raincoat, in the act of climbing in through the window which he has managed to force open.

Rada's voice returns to me as I knock off the safety catch of my pistol and level it at him as she taught me, easing the trigger, trying not to jerk it in panic. The blast is deafening in the confined space, making my ears ring, but the result is even more shocking to me. The man's body jumps, and blood spurts from a hole that has appeared where the bullet has ripped through his clothes. But he has not stopped; his head turns to look at me, an expression of pain and anger and hate on his face, and he hastens to get his foot on the floor. I fire another shot, then two more, until he slumps limply on the window frame, one arm and one leg hanging inside, his blood running down the wall beneath the sill.

Olgha arrives beside me, and we run together to the window and heave the body out, watching it bounce off the roof of the woodstore and disappear from sight.

As Olgha closes the window, a crash from the next room alerts us, and we run back out into the hallway. I am slightly ahead of Olgha, and reach the door just as the shadowy silhouette of a man emerges from the room opposite. I only have time to register a brown jacket and grey beard before he leaps at me with grasping hands, knocking my gun from my hands before I can raise it to shoot. He grabs me, spinning me around and gripping me in a bear hug, pressing a knife to my throat. I see Olgha stoop to pick up the gun and point it, but the man is holding me as a shield and she dares not fire.

"Drop the gun," he shouts at her, jabbing the point of the knife against my skin. I think I feel it penetrate the flesh, and warm blood trickling down my neck.

She does as instructed, glaring at him. Then I see her expression change to a kind of smile, and at the same moment, the man's grip on me loosens, the knife dropping from his hand and thudding onto the rug at my feet. I twist free and turn to see what is happening.

Max is standing behind the man, towering over him, his huge hands around the man's neck, squeezing the life out of him. "Not hurt my Natalie," he says as the man collapses, his face purple, his tongue lolling from his mouth.

Olgha picks up the gun again, and hands it to me. "You have to finish him," she shouts above the din from downstairs, where guns are still firing, and Malchik, the dog, is barking and growling like a wild animal.

"I can't shoot a helpless man," I answer, pathetically.

"Then give it to me and I will," she orders, holding out her hand.

"No," I reply, vehemently, but then a flurry of shots and shouts from downstairs interrupts us.

As I run to the top of the stairs, followed by Olgha and, more slowly, Max, the gunfire and barking stops, and a silence falls that is even more ominous. We begin to descend, and when I can see into the kitchen I observe that the door is open, swinging in the wind that is driving rain through like waves crashing on a shore. Two men are standing just inside, and the bodies of Stefan, Rada, and the dog are lying on the floor, puddles of blood forming beneath each of them. As I watch, one of the men kicks the dog, then starts to lean over Stefan's still form.

He is stopped, however, by his associate, who lets out a yell when he sees Olgha and me, and he runs past the other man towards the stairs. I raise my pistol and aim at him, but then I see that the other one is pointing a gun at me, so I switch aim and start firing at him, one shot then another until a click tells me that my gun is empty. The man with the gun has fallen, but the other stands grinning in triumph, snatching up the weapon and raising it. I throw my useless gun at him, but it falls short, and I see the muzzle of his pistol staring at me.

The shot that I hear, however, does not come from his gun, but from the floor beside him, where Rada has propped herself up on one elbow and is lying on her side, her pistol still smoking.

The man drops, blood pumping from a hole in his neck where the bullet has passed right through. I can see that Rada is injured, a large red stain spreading into her shirt around her left shoulder, and she looks pale and in pain, but I am glad to see her moving.

Olgha and I begin to run down the last few steps, but are amazed when Rada turns her gun and points it at our heads.

"Rada, it's me, Natalie," I say lamely, stopping at the foot of the stairs. I wonder if perhaps she cannot not see clearly, or is confused by the pain.

She lowers the gun, and I relax, but then she does what seems to me to be a strange thing: looking past us and smiling, grimly, she nods her head. Puzzled, I start to turn, to see what she is looking at, but before I have completed the movement there is a bumping sound, and something bounces past us, glancing against my legs and knocking me off my feet like a skittle.

As I land on my hands and knees I find that, on the floor beside me, lies the body of the man Max strangled outside the bedroom. I look up to the top of the stairs, where Max is standing on the landing, grinning and theatrically brushing his hands together, as though knocking dust from them. The man had apparently somehow recovered enough to have one more try at us, but as he lies there on the floor beside us, his neck now at an odd angle, he will clearly not trouble us again.

Chapter 31

~ Aftermath ~

The stone slabs that make up the kitchen floor are awash with blood and rainwater, and I tread carefully past Malchik's still form as I cross the room to close and bolt the door. At the same time, Olgha hurries to Stefan's side and begins to examine him. Rada is sitting on the wet floor, her back against the sideboard, and I kneel by her side to examine her wound. Though bloody and messy, it does not seem to be life-threatening. It appears that the bullet must have passed right through the flesh of her arm, just below her shoulder. She has lost quite a lot of blood, and the bullet may have nicked the bone, but it could have been a lot worse.

I use Rada's own knife to cut away her shirt sleeve, then tear the material into strips for bandages with which to bind the wound tightly, to stem the flow of blood. When I am sure she is stable, I leave her in Max's care while I go to help Olgha.

Stefan's condition is much worse; he is badly injured and unconscious. Hit in the chest and abdomen by two bullets, he is bleeding heavily. We did not dare try to move him, so we dress his wounds as best we can where he lies on the floor, then cover him with blankets to keep him warm. Though I can see tears running down her cheeks, Olgha's face is frozen into an expression of determination, her lips tightly pressed together, all emotion suppressed so that she can concentrate on treating her husband.

"He needs a doctor," I say, gently.

"I know," she replies, shaking her head, "but I cannot

leave him to bring one."

"This has all happened because of me," I comment. "I am so sorry for bringing it upon you."

She shrugs, but says nothing.

"Who is your nearest neighbour?" I ask.

She points to the east. "Cherenkov, about half an hour's walk."

I feel guilty, and need to redeem myself. "I will go and tell them," I say.

She nods. "Thank you."

* * *

It is still raining hard, so I take a waterproof coat down from the row of hooks beside the door. But as I am putting it on, there is the sound of horses hooves clattering into the cobbled yard outside. I run to peep carefully out of the broken window, in time to see the shadowy shapes of three armed men dismounting in the wet gloom of the driving rain.

"More of Avadeyev's men?" I moan incredulously to Rada, who also heard the horses and has struggled to her feet to stand beside me. "Is this how it is to be forever, pursued day and night?"

She already has her rifle in her hand, a grim expression on her face, and passes me her spare pistol, for mine is at the bottom of the stairs, still empty.

But Olgha joins us and places a hand on my arm.

"Wait!" she says. "These are our neighbours. Don't shoot!"

She opens the door to admit them, calling out their names. Rada and I put our guns down and join her. The men come into the kitchen, water dripping from their coats, and look at the scene of carnage around the kitchen with amazement.

"This is Boris," Olgha informs me, "and his sons Georgy and Nikolay."

The elder of the three men looks at me and inclines his head once in response.

"We heard gunshots, and came to help," he explains to Olgha. "What has been happening?"

"We think they came for me," I tell him. "Stefan is badly hurt." I point to where Olgha has returned to kneel at her husband's side, arranging the blanket around him.

Boris turns to one of his sons. "Nikolay, ride like the wind and bring the doctor."

The man nods, and departs at once.

"Who are you?" Boris asks me, gruffly.

His caution is understandable; he has never seen me before, and here I have brought disaster to his friends.

I point to Max. "The man that Stefan and Olgha saved is my fiancé. His name is Max, and I am Natalie, his wife-to-be." Then I point to the corpses. "We were on the run from those men, but they followed me here and attacked us."

He looks around the room. "Georgy and I will help you to clean up in here," he says.

Rada is also keen to help, but she is pale and unsteady from the loss of blood. Olgha instructs her to go upstairs and rest in one of the spare bedrooms. I ask Max to take her, as someone to lean on, and to make sure that she obeys.

Boris and Georgy begin to drag the bodies of our two attackers outside and across the yard. They lay them on some straw in a clear part of the barn, adding those that lay scattered around the yard, and the one from the back of the house ~ seven, in all. I carry out the body of poor Malchik, who died bravely trying to save his family, and lay it beside them. They will all have to be buried tomorrow. We

207

stack their weapons in a corner of the barn.

Max returns to the kitchen after escorting Rada to bed, and stands by the stairs looking lost. I can see that he longs to help, but he is slow to move. Eventually, Boris asks him to help him to nail some boards over the broken window, while I mop and dry the kitchen floor and Olgha takes a moment away from her husband to put some soup on the stove to heat.

* * *

Now we are done with the tidying up, and outside the rain has eased to a drizzle. Night has fallen, and as the clouds roll away to the east, the moon and stars have appeared ~ the world has eased itself, exhausted, out of its tantrum. We have closed up the barn and are now congregating in the kitchen. As the men enter, I take their wet coats from them and hang them on the rail near the fire to dry, and Olgha starts to serve the soup that she has prepared for us.

We have scarcely sat at the table, however, when I am amazed to hear Nikolay return, less than an hour after leaving. Puzzled, I join his father and brother in the yard as they greet him. "Surely you have not ridden all the way to Nizhny and back in such a short time," I exclaim as he dismounts.

Boris laughs. "Doctor Losev works one of the farms a little way to the south," he informs me. "The city doctors will not come out here, to this barbarous countryside. And even if they did we could not afford their fancy prices. Losev knows how hard our lives are, because he shares it. He cares for us all, humans and animals, and accepts payment in produce or whatever we can give for his services. It is how we farmers survive."

"He is on his way," Nikolay advises us. "He should be

here within an hour."

It is a huge relief that help will soon arrive for Stefan and Rada. "Thank you all for what you are doing," I say to the three men as we turn to head back into the kitchen. "This is what I thought the revolution was supposed to be delivering to all citizens, co-operation and an end to privilege, but instead it is just a continuation of the old ways under different rulers."

Boris nods. "City people with city ways," he grunts.

And that is the truth; he has summed it up in one simple phrase. The city way is to try to make everyone the same, to fit into the system, whereas these country people have discovered how to live with their differences and to turn them to the advantage of all.

Back indoors, we return to the kitchen table to resume our soup and bread.

* * *

An hour has passed. Boris and his sons have left, promising to return tomorrow morning to help dig and fill the graves. As they disappear through the opening in the wall, the doctor arrives, driving a buggy. Max takes his horse and begins to unharness it from the shafts of the cart, and the doctor hurries indoors, carrying a large leather Gladstone bag.

He kneels on the hard stone floor and examines Stefan, removing the pads with which Olgha has stemmed the flow of blood, and cutting away some of Stefan's clothes. I bring him a cushion to kneel on, for which he thanks me, absently, as he contemplates Stefan's injuries.

After five minutes he pronounces that the wound in Stefan's abdomen, though it looks bad, is not serious in itself. The bullet has sliced across his belly at an angle, damaging a lot of surface flesh, but without striking any of his internal organs. He cleans it and stitches it closed.

Stefan's chest wound, however, is a greater test of the doctor's skills. In a process similar to that which I saw when I watched Max's bullet being removed, Losev carefully plucks out the offending missile from where it has lodged against one of Stefan's ribs, and the pieces of material carried in with the projectile, then cleans out the hole with disinfectant. Finally, he stitches it up and applies a dressing.

"His rib prevented the bullet from penetrating to his lung," he declares as he stands up and stretches. "There are no internal organs damaged. But it is the shock caused by the sudden loss of blood that concerns me most. Fortunately, he is strong, and there is a good chance of recovery. It is likely that he will regain consciousness before the night is through. Give him some water to drink, and a little soup if he can manage it. Keep him warm."

"Can we make him more comfortable, Losev?" Olgha asks. "It does not seem good that he is laying on a cold, hard floor."

The doctor purses his lips. "Really, we should not try to move him. But you are right, and we could shift him with care. Do you have something we could put under him?"

"Yes," Olgha replies. "A thin mattress." She looks to Max. "You know the one?"

He nods, and I follow him up the stairs to help. When we return, we bring Rada with us for the doctor to check. Losev examines her shoulder, redresses it, and pronounces that he sees no cause for concern there.

We lay the mattress beside Stefan, and the doctor supervises while the rest of us carefully work a blanket under him. Then, with all of us gripping the corners and sides of the blanket, we lift it and ease him onto the mattress, finally rearranging his blankets over him again.

The doctor is pleased. "Good, now do not allow him to get up for anything. If he needs to pass water or empty his bowel, he must do it here, and you will have to help him." He fixes Olgha with a stare and raised eyebrows, to make sure she understands his meaning.

She manages a tight smile. "He will do as I tell him, doctor."

Losev also smiles, reassuringly. "I am confident he will soon be on his feet and back to his normal, grumpy self." He fumbles in his bag and withdraws a small brown bottle, which he hands to Olgha. "This is morphine. If the pain is bad, put a drop on his tongue. I will return tomorrow afternoon to check on him."

At this cue, Max goes ahead of Losev into the yard and leads the doctor's horse from the stable, where it has enjoyed a brief rest and some hay, and begins to harness it to the buggy. In moments, Losev is ready to leave, and we have all gathered at the kitchen door to watch and wave as he turns the corner of the buildings and vanishes from our sight.

It is near to midnight when we close and lock the kitchen door, and though I suspect that none of us will be able to sleep, we agree that we should at least try. I have instructed Rada to go back to bed, and she is so exhausted that she has amazed me by agreeing without argument.

As she wearily climbs the stairs, Max and I move two armchairs across the room ~ one so that Olgha can sit beside Stefan, and another one for me. I will stay with them, my pistol in my lap, to keep guard.

Max kisses me and holds me tight, then makes his way back upstairs. I push some more logs into the fire in the big cooking stove and close its door, before settling down next to Olgha for the night.

Chapter 32

~ *Tuesday 3rd September 1918* ~

A fine sentry I have proved to be! A hand on my shoulder gently shakes me awake in the darkness, and for a few seconds I am confused as to where I am. Rada's voice comes from the figure that is standing beside me:

"It's only me, Nata," she whispers. "It's six o'clock. Go and join Max, I'll take over here."

I push myself out of the soft chair and carefully hug her, then she takes the gun from my hand and settles into the armchair, while I carefully climb the shadowy stairs.

I find the room with Max in, and quietly undress. But as I slip into bed beside him he senses my arrival, and curls his big arm around me, pulling me close. I nestle into the warmth of his body, remembering the first night we spent together at his sister's café in Yekaterinberg. I hear in my head again the song he sang to me, a Ukranian love song. I do not know the words, properly, so I just quietly hum the tune.

Then an amazing thing happens ~ he joins in, singing the words I recognise: "Oy u Hayu, Pry Dunayu."

Tears spring to my eyes. He remembers! His mind is not permanently damaged. He will recover, and I will help him.

We belong together, and together we will build our new future.

* * *

To my joy and relief, Stefan is awake and cogent when we come downstairs to join the others soon after sunrise.

213

Though weak, he is enquiring about the events after he was shot. As we recount everything to him, he sips some soup, and soon afterwards, falls asleep again.

As soon as possible, Rada and I leave the others and go out to the barn. Before Boris and his sons arrive, I am anxious to learn more about the men sent to attack the farmhouse. So we begin searching through the pockets of the gunmen.

We find very little, but what we find is significant; Rada has come up with something, a letter. Her eyebrows rise as she read it.

"Well, this is a surprise," she says, passing it to me.

It reads, simply:

> **The traitor Tereshchenko will be in Nizhny Novgorod on 1st September. She must not live.**

It carries no names, only a cryptic symbol at its head, a representation of a shining sun with the words 'Pure' above it, and 'White' beneath.

"Pure White?" I say, wrinkling my face in puzzlement. "So they were Whites, nothing to do with Avadeyev."

"Apparently."

But who are the 'Pure Whites'?"

"I have heard of them," she replies. "They are an extremist resistance group, hostile to the Bolsheviks, supported by the royal families of foreign monarchies. There are said to be still a few Romanovs alive in hiding, and the Pure Whites plan to put one back in control of Russia."

We take the letter indoors and show it to Olgha, who is still keeping vigil beside her sleeping husband. After she has read it, Rada repeats what she just told me.

"There are rumours that a member of the royal family survived the massacre," Olgha comments. "Some say it is the princess Anastasia."

I shake my head; it is time for me to disclose my own little bomb-shell; there are to be no secrets from my new family. "No, it was me, Olgha. Very few people know this, and I wish it was otherwise, but I am half royal ~ a bastard. I never knew my father, but I have learnt that he was one of the Tsar's brothers. When he was killed in a naval battle in the war against Japan, the Empress took me in. It was never admitted that I shared their royal blood, and I only found out last year. It's the reason I was with them when they were murdered, and why Max and I have been on the run from Avadeyev ever since. What I don't understand is how this 'Pure White' organisation knows about me, and why they want me dead so badly."

"Could they have been the ones who were trying to kill you in Moscow, when you joined Aleksandra?" Rada suggests.

"Why yes, of course!" I exclaim. "That explains a lot. I have been assuming that Avadeyev was behind all the attempts on my life, but some, or perhaps even most, of them must have been these 'Pure Whites'. And now I think of it, I suspect that the woman who claimed to be my mother was actually working for them. Yes! They probably had Sacha's mother in on it, too. I mean, it was bad enough that I refused to become their figure-head, but to then compound it by going to work for the Bolsheviks must have seemed like a betrayal. No wonder they want to kill me."

* * *

Mid-morning and, true to their word, Boris and his sons have arrived and laboured in the field beside the farmhouse, digging eight graves, including a small one for Malchik, the brave little dog who died trying to protect us.

Now we are gathered around the row of graves, each with its unknown occupant, to show respect for the dead. Misguided though they were, and murderously fanatical about their cause, we agree that their souls are now in the care of whatever deity they may have believed in. For my part, although I do not have a god to pray to, I respect their passion and bravery, and I stand in respectful silence as Boris chants a burial dirge.

It has started to rain again. Not the deluge of yesterday, but a steady drizzle that shrouds the world in a kind of grey mist. We return to the farmhouse for some warm food before the men leave to return to their own farm. We have given them the weapons of our dead attackers, by way of thanks for their help. They can keep them or sell them; we have no need of any more guns ~ we have a veritable arsenal of our own ~ and we want to give them something to show our gratitude.

* * *

Olgha and I are feeding and cleaning out the animals when the doctor returns. After examining the two patients, he declares that he is pleased with both of them, though he warns us to be scrupulous in cleaning the wounds. With much argument, he finally consents to let Stefan climb the stairs to sleep in his own bed, supported by Olgha and Max, but is insistent that he must not do any physical work for at least a week.

Rada and I have talked privately, and offered to stay to help Stefan and Olgha for as long as they need us. We will work, doing what Stefan is unable to do for a while, helping with the harvest and the animals and around the house.

216

If it is true what Avadeyev told me (and why would he bother to lie when he was about to kill me?) Sverdlov is not expecting me to survive this trip. As far as the Party is concerned, I was an inconvenience that has been eliminated. I am sure that Aleksandra will miss me, will probably be sad, and may be suspicious about my disappearance, but no doubt Sverdlov will have answers for her. In their minds, I have ceased to exist. Rada's absence could also be connected to my non-return, and they already know that Nina was injured (or killed) in the confrontation with Avadeyev's men outside the cafe. We are free to blend into the countryside, to finally leave the past behind and start a new life.

~ Finale ~

The sleek limousine, with its darkened windows, merged smoothly and silently into the early-morning rush hour traffic, like a black shark slipping into a shoal of unsuspecting, shimmering silvery fishes. Despite my nerves, I couldn't help smiling at the lady beside me in the back of the car. She was as excited as a child, her age forgotten, twisting in her seat to look first one way and then the other, turning her head, pushing her glasses back on her nose as they slipped down again, pointing out landmarks she recognised, and chattering almost incessantly as memories flowed from her in a torrent.

"That's the Winter Palace! Look, over there! And Palace Square! And the railway station! The main one, for the Trans-Russia Railway, you know, the one that goes right across to Siberia and China. We came through here when . . . . ," her voice trailed off as she remembered one of the less happy memories.

The lady was my grandmother, Natalie Tereshchenko. After sixty-six years away, she was back in the country of her childhood, Russia. It was August 1985, and we were being driven through the beautiful city of Saint Petersburg (also known for a while as Petrograd and then, for many years, Leningrad) on our way to Pushkin, the town that used to be called Tsarskoye Selo. We were riding in a luxurious, chauffeur-driven limousine provided for us by the Russian leader, Mikhail Gorbachev. Our destination, on the edge of Tsarskoye Selo, was the Alexander Palace, once the home of Nicholas II, the last Tsar of Russia, and his family, where Natalie had lived and worked when she was a young woman.

Our journey had started a year earlier, when I received a surprise phone call from my grandmother to ask if I would help her to make a nostalgic trip back to her former home. She had been so excited about her plan, to return one last time to see the palace where she grew up, and it was important to her that she took one of the women in the family with her. My mother ~ her daughter Audrey ~ was too frail after her illness, so she asked me, Elizabeth, her granddaughter, spinster of this parish, to take the trip with her.

To me she was always Nana Shengo (I was unable to pronounce her name properly when, as a little girl, I would beg my parents to take me to see Nana and Granddad). Every visit to their cottage was like a fairytale, and I would sit silently listening to Nan's magical stories about princesses and palaces, dukes and princes, and always about Max.

Granddad Max was a gentle man with a mass of unruly blonde hair above an angular face, with strong cheekbones and a proud jaw. Even in his later years, he was tall, straight-backed and strong. Their love was as evident then as it must have been all those years before, and I had never heard a bad word pass between them. He died of pneumonia following a bout of influenza in 1980, and Nana Shengo withdrew from almost all contact with the outside world. It was heartbreaking to see the way she shrank, like a balloon the day after a party, as though all purpose had been sucked from her life. For three years she hid in her little cottage, refusing to see anyone but her closest family.

Then, on her eighty-third birthday, on the twentieth of February nineteen eighty-four, she found her old diaries in the back of a drawer, and made a decision to go back to the place that held so many memories. It was there that she was taken in as a baby by the Empress Alexandra, wife of The Tsar of Russia, and there, at the age of sixteen, that she became Lady-in-Waiting to Tatiana, the second of the four royal daughters.

Once the decision was made, Nan and I talked every day on the phone, and I visited her many times, to work out plans and write letters with her, and it was good to see the old sparkle return to her eyes. We knew it would take quite a lot to set up the trip, but we soon discovered that there were many more obstacles than we had thought possible.

Of course, at that time there were no package holidays to Russia, which was isolated from the rest of the world by the aggressive posturing of successive governments ~ on both sides of the Iron Curtain ~ and we figured that getting permission to even enter Russia would involve complicated procedures that were hard to understand. As it turned out, we were right, but in ways we could not have anticipated.

We started by writing to the British Foreign Office for advice on how to set about it. The people there were, to say the least, lukewarm about the plan, and offered little advice. For a while we wondered if it was possible at all, but were determined not to give up.

So we wrote to our Prime Minister at the time, Mrs Thatcher, and to the then Russian leader, Secretary Chernenko. We had read in the newspapers that Mr Chernenko was ill, so we were not surprised when we did not receive an answer.

But Nan did receive a reply from Mrs Thatcher, saying that she would ask her Foreign Secretary, Geoffrey Howe, to contact the Kremlin and ask for their assistance. We thought that things might get moving after that, but weeks passed and, apart from a letter from Mr Howe, saying that he had not received any reply from Russia, nothing happened.

We had begun to think that the whole project was impossible when, in May 1985, we unexpectedly received a letter from Russia, signed by the new Russian leader, Mikhail Gorbachev, authorising our visit and promising his support. What a shock! Apparently, all the letters relating to our request to visit Russia had been pushed under a pile of more important items by a clerk in the General Secretary's office, and only came to light when Mr Gorbachev succeeded Chernenko as the supreme leader of that huge country. It seems that one of the secretaries assigned the task of clearing the backlog of paperwork had taken an interest in the content of the letters, and drawn Mr Gorbachev's attention to them.

Once Mr Gorbachev became involved, the Russian authorities seemed also to enter into the spirit of the venture. They started to help us in many unexpected ways, with arranging visas and permits and booking hotel rooms and arranging transport and security for us at the Russian end.

And after that, the Foreign Office also became amazingly helpful, and guided us through the steps to all the UK arrangements that were involved. I had the impression that neither side wanted to be outdone by the other, and that we had become a kind of project for everybody. Each department suddenly seemed to have taken an almost proprietorial interest in making sure it all went smoothly.

~ Russia ~

And so it was that, on the twenty-sixth of August nineteen eighty-five, ironically the anniversary of her journey from Alexander Palace into exile in Tobolsk, we stepped from a plane into the long, late afternoon shadows at Pulkovo airport, in Russia's second city, Petrograd. We cleared customs and passport control without incident (Nan's rusty Russian came in handy), and emerged into the airport arrivals lounge, where we saw the name 'Tereshchenko' printed boldly on a large card being held aloft by a tall, smartly-dressed man.

He introduced himself as Sergey Cherenkov. He spoke English in clipped sentences, with a very strong Russian accent, and interspersed with many "er"'s and "mm"s and rolling "rrr"s, which made it hard for me to understand what he said (though I found it very sexy). Nan, apparently, had no problem comprehending him. His appearance was so obviously intended to be unobtrusive that he stood out in the crowd, like a red bus among black taxis. He wore a dark suit, white shirt and grey tie, and I noticed that his shoes were gleaming. The letters KGB came to mind, but I scolded myself for being cynical.

"I am your guiding, ladies and gentleman ... (mmm) ... Please give by our glorrrious leader, Chairman Gorrrbachev ... (mmm) ... and with his best wish," he said, as though reciting a passage from a public information leaflet. "Any you help durrring ... (mmm) ... staying, please ... (er) ... talk me, and I will ... (mmm) ... arranging it for her."

We smiled nervously and thanked him.

With a small bow, he led us out of the building and

across a wide pavement to where a sleek, black, chauffeur-driven limousine was waiting, with a small grey flag fluttering on the bonnet, featuring the distinctive Hammer and Sickle emblem in red. The chauffeur leapt out and held open the rear door for us, and we sank into deep leather seats and smelt the sweet, cool, conditioned air.

As the car took us through wide streets between tall skyscrapers to our hotel, I noticed that Petrograd seemed to have few old buildings, and I commented on this to Sergey.

"Yes. The Nazis bomb-bed and ... (mmm) ... shells ... (mmm) ... the city for many days to the war," he explained. "Much of the houses was destroyed, and also much history buildings. A big ... (erm) ... vosstanovleniye?"

"Reconstruction," Nan offered.

"Da, yes, dank you. A big ... rrre-con-strook-shon ... is made when the war is end. Some we have ... (mmm) ... repaired ... but also much lost."

I was struck by the cleanliness everywhere in the city, and also by the huge number of statues and monuments, as the limousine, with its little fluttering flag, drove sedately through the traffic. Here was a nation anxiously proclaiming its successes, urging its people to be patriotic, as though it felt that the world would find it lacking otherwise.

* * *

Eventually the chauffeur brought us to a halt outside the Hotel Moika, a beautiful, elegant, old, four-storey hotel in the centre of the city, overlooking the river. This was the hotel chosen for us by the Russian leader, and paid for by the government; it seemed that he wanted to impress us, as if we were special guests (though I knew that, of course, it was just Nan who was special). If this building had been damaged in the war, then clearly, no expense had been spared since to restore it to its former glory and create a feeling of complete luxury.

The floor of the spacious entrance area was thickly carpeted and the walls were decorated in traditional style, with gigantic paintings and ornate mouldings, and draped with heavy velvet curtains. We were greeted at a huge, beautifully carved, mahogany reception desk by smartly uniformed staff.

The chauffeur carried our bags in for us, and Sergey stayed with us as we checked in. He told us that preparations had been made for him to meet us in the morning and take us to the palace, then he bade us a good night.

A hotel porter (nice, but not talkative) took our bags and led us up to our room, which turned out to be an elegant suite on the fourth floor, beautifully decorated, with more draped curtains, more thick, luxurious carpets, and large windows that looked out over the river. We had separate bedrooms, each with a four-poster bed and private shower room.

After the porter had left, Nan and I stood together in the lounge and looked out of the window, with its wonderful view of the river and out across the rooftops of the city. The evening was still and warm, and the sun was just settling down towards the horizon on our right, surrounded by an explosion of red and orange and purple clouds which were reflected in the water. We looked at each other and smiled.

"We made it, Nan," I said.

She slowly let out her breath, relaxing at last. "Thank you for everything, Elizabeth dear," she said, emotionally.

"Hey, you did it all," I grinned, I'm just here for the holiday."

She took my hand in hers and raised it to her face and held it there for a moment, deep in contemplation. "I am very nervous, you know," she said quietly.

"Of course, who wouldn't be. But look, the hard part is behind you now, tomorrow you will finally meet up with your past. Who knows, we might see the young Natalie, walking the corridors of the palace, waiting for you to return."

She smiled. "What an imagination you have, Elizabeth!"

* * *

After dinner in the grand dining hall that filled the basement area of the hotel, we returned to our suite and, for a while, we chatted about the flight, the day just finishing and the day to come. We ordered some coffee, then sat in the huge settee near the window.

"What was it like to work for the family?" I asked.

She smiled, wryly, and settled back into the cushions. She had told me the stories about her childhood so many times that I could almost recite them word for word, but she knew that I still loved to hear her talk about those days. "The Empress was good to her ladies, and kind to me," she replied. "But I was treated differently from the other staff; I was educated with the duchesses, and allowed to attend functions with the family. I didn't understand why, at the time, but I seemed to enjoy a different status to everyone else ~ not part of the family, but more than just a servant. Alexandra didn't love me, I knew that, but she treated me well, though my special treatment caused resentment among the other staff. I was between stations, never wholly one thing or the other; it made me feel quite alone."

She lapsed into her memories, and was quiet for a while. I was used to this, too, and waited patiently.

"Alexandra was a complex woman," she finally said quietly, "fanatically religious, and strong-willed. Most of us were aware that she was the power behind the throne; she always got her own way, and Nicholas hardly made any decisions without first consulting her.

"Despite her dismissive attitude to the aspirations of the masses, she wanted to be seen as a good leader ~ her German upbringing again, I suppose. The trouble was, she thought she knew what the people needed better than they did themselves, and she believed that they wanted to be ruled with a firm hand. She could not comprehend that many of the ordinary citizens deeply resented the royal family's ostentatious wealth and power, when they themselves were starving and unable to control their own lives.

"And they were incompetent! She and Nicholas made terrible, ignorant mistakes in the running of the country. They had a kind of arrogance that they were superior to everything and everyone, and they built up a bad reputation for causing the deaths of huge numbers of people. Did you know that Nicholas was called 'Nicholas The Bloody' by some people, after the killings of dissenters and the dreadful losses on the battlefields against Japan and Germany?"

I shook my head. I hadn't known, but it came as no real surprise. I knew from my research that Russia had been ruled, often with greed and cruelty, by the Romanov family for hundreds of years, and that their popularity had declined seriously by the time Nan arrived at the palace. There had been some very bad lapses of judgement and leadership by several generations.

"But, you know," she continued, "they were just born into the myth about royalty that had been constructed over generations, that they were granted their status by God and were entitled to it by birth. Maybe they had to believe it, otherwise they would have been forced to see that it was a sham and to give up their luxurious lifestyle. It was easy for me to see that the girls had already been indoctrinated with the same nonsense."

She always called them The Girls ~ it was quaint and rather touching ~ but, actually, most of the princesses were older than her. Olga, the eldest, was 22 when she died, Tatiana was 20 and Maria was 19. Only Anastasia was younger than the eighteen-year-old Natalie who fled from the slaughter in the basement of the house in Yekaterinberg.

I wanted to hear more, but by then we were both finding our eyelids drooping. We were exhausted from our long day, and soon we bid each other goodnight and went to our bedrooms. Two very tired ladies went straight to bed and slept solidly.

~ Catherine Palace ~

Soon after dawn the next morning we were up and enjoying a little walk along the river in the chilly, early-morning sunlight. The air was clean and the sun, low on the horizon to our left, sparkled on the ripples as we sat on the concrete wall above the river and watched boats chugging and splashing back and forth.

Eventually, though, the cold penetrated our inadequate clothes, and we returned to the hotel for a hot shower, then took the lift down to the dining room for breakfast. We were just finishing when Sergey came to our table to inform us that he had arrived, then he waited in the foyer while we returned to our rooms for our handbags and coats.

A quick check in the mirror, and we headed back to the lift and down to the entrance hall again. Nan looked very smart in a pastel blue blouse, navy blue dress with light grey rectangles dotted over it, and a patent navy blue belt and matching shoes. Around her neck was a silver chain, with a pale turquiose stone in a silver mount. Over the dress, she wore a white, lightweight jacket. I had chosen a silver-grey trouser suit with a white blouse, and black shoes with a small heel.

At the front doors of the hotel, just before following Sergey out to the waiting car, we stopped spontaneously, and looked at each other. We both smiled.

"Are you ready for this?" I asked.

She nodded, biting her bottom lip.

"Let's do it, then."

The chauffeur helped us into the car with Sergey, and we set off through the wide streets of the city. After a while, the car merged onto a motorway, through a sweeping curved access road, and began to speed along the highway that would take Nan into her past.

* * *

Half an hour later, we turned off the wide, multi-lane artery onto a lesser vein, and then ever smaller roads, eventually passing through a small town and then parkland. Here we stopped at a pair of massive iron gates, beside which waited an open military vehicle, like a Jeep, with an officer and two smartly dressed soldiers sitting in it. Nan and I stayed in the car, peering past our silent and impassive chauffeur, watching as Sergey spoke quietly in Russian with the officer. Then he returned to the car and we followed the Jeep through the gates and into the grounds. The gates were opened for us by a soldier, but as we passed through there was also a red and white barrier, which had been raised, and a pair of grey sentry boxes, manned by armed guards, who watched us with curiosity.

The two vehicles travelled slowly along an avenue through beautiful parkland. Nan had fallen silent, and I looked at her anxiously; she had become pensive ~ it seemed to me that her mind was reliving days, long ago, when her life was very different.

The park was immense, but neglected. Rolling acres of overgrown lawns were spread on both sides, with trees that had clearly been arranged precisely to achieve maximum effect ~ here a single oak, there a chestnut, over there a clump of birch. In some places, there were large areas of woodland, where I could imagine royal hunting parties out for a day's sport, and in others, pretty little pagodas peeped at us from leafy hideaways. It was mid-morning on a bright, beautiful late-August day, and the sun gleamed on colourful bushes, alive with flowers.

230

After what seemed an age, but in reality was only a few minutes, we turned a wide, sweeping bend, and a huge, ancient building swung into view. From the window on my side of the car it looked magnificent, a symbol of a kind of affluence that would only be enjoyed today by business tycoons and some overpaid celebrities. "There it is!" I cried, feeling like a child as the words shot out.

Sergey smiled. "No, devushka, that is the Catherine Palace. It is much as grand of Alexander Palace."

"May we visit it, please?" asked Nan, suddenly alert again.

"Of course."

He spoke to the driver, who picked up a device from his dashboard, like a telephone handset, and rattled off something in Russian, receiving a swift reply which he relayed to Sergey.

"We will soon meet another road ~ it is going to the Catherine Palace," Sergey told us.

And indeed, within a minute or two, the car took a fork in the road and shortly pulled up beside the impressive building. Closer to, I could see that there was scaffolding erected across the centre of it, and quite a number of people were hard at work.

Our smart military escort, in their long grey coats with crimson piping, jumped from their Jeep and waited for us, while our chauffeur opened our door.

We stepped out into the sunshine, suddenly warm after the air conditioned car.

Catherine Palace was a long building, stretching away to our right and left, looking for all the world like a grand parade of terrace houses. It rose three floors, with entrances and balconies protruding at intervals along its length. There was gold in excess, and bright colours fought for attention like children in a classroom.

Sergey came to stand beside us as we looked.

"The German army it is here in the war, for a head- ... (mmm) ... -quarter, after he captures Staligrad. When they go, they made big fire," he said, simply, with sadness in his face.

And we could see some of the damage. Apart from the area at the centre, where considerable restoration work had already taken place, much of the building was clearly fire damaged: many of the windows were just gaping holes, and smoke-blackened smudges rose from each to stain the once-elegant façade.

Sergey led us, accompanied by our escort, towards an entrance hidden amidst the scaffolding. Some workers stopped to watch us, and some words were exchanged. "They say to be ... (mmm) ... caring? No ... careful ... because much not safe," he explained.

Close up it was beautiful. As far as I could see, the external reconstruction work in this section was finished, and the workers were painting the walls a light shade of blue, and the window frames white ~ rather like some Wedgwood pottery I had seen. Here and there were tall, sturdy columns, with beautifully carved stone statues at the base of each, and at every door and window were gold cherubs and ornamental scrolls and crests.

"The family hardly ever used this palace," said Nan, unexpectedly, looking up and around her. "They preferred the cosier Alexander Palace. This was reserved for state occasions and an occasional ball."

We followed Sergey inside, and found ourselves in a large room, where more restoration was taking place. Here, murals were being painstakingly cleaned and repainted, and ornamental door frames erected.

"This was an anteroom to the State Dining Room," Nan informed us, suddenly talkative, becoming our unofficial guide, "where the Russian royal family showed off their wealth to other royal families. There would be an orchestra playing over there ..." she waved her stick towards a far corner, "... as the Tsar and Empress greeted guests here at the door. And tables were laid out with hors d'ouvre along both sides, there."

It was stunning in its ostentatious beauty; beautiful marble tiles covered the floor, a mural depicting a battle scene covered one wall, and gold ornamentation dripped from every window frame and the ceiling above us like melting candle-wax. But it was so overstated, so garish, that its effect on me was not to inspire awe, but rather, to my amazement, I was sickened by it. I found that I could understand the resentment felt by the ordinary Russian citizens at the ostentatious wealth and power of this privileged few, who had so much while they had little or nothing. The strength of that feeling, and its sudden manifestation, surprised me. All at once I knew what Nan had tried to explain to me. How it had driven the masses to revolt against the monarchy and aristocracy, not just in Russia, but in France too, a hundred years earlier.

After studying it in pensive silence for a while, we followed the long, worn carpet through the centre of the room (there to protect the floor from the feet of the many workers passing back and forth) into an even larger hall, where, again, the mural painters were at work, and carpenters were busy building a huge table.

"Ah, this is the State Dining Room," Nan declared.

The table under construction was enormous, big enough to seat fifty people. Nan waved her arm in a big sweep, warming to her topic, and nearly catching Sergey with her stick as it hurtled past his head.

"The original table had an amazing system. Beside each place setting there was a round slate, and a guest would write on the slate what they wanted to eat, anything that came to mind, then ring a bell beside it. The slate would disappear down into the table, and a little later would come back up again with whatever the guest had ordered." A smile suddenly pulled at her mouth. "Or, sometimes, what someone else had ordered," she giggled.

"Ladies and gentlemen . . . ," began Sergey.

"Sergey, darling," Nan interrupted. "Forgive me for correcting you, but just 'ladies' will do. You are the only gentleman here." She smiled sweetly at him. The change in her demeanor was amazing; she was on home ground.

He became flustered. "(mmm) ... Thank you. I am learn only English now, not ... (erm) ... many."

He was blushing. I wasn't sure, but I think he was more embarrassed at being called 'darling' than at having his broken English corrected.

"Devushka, will you like follow me? There is more to see." He gestured towards a door at the end of the dining hall, the frame of which was being fitted with more carved, golden mouldings, and we followed him through into a modest room with a wide staircase rising to our left. However, this was not our destination, apparently, for we passed straight on and through another door into a huge hall.

"The Great Ballroom," sighed Nan, a small smile again on her lips. Her eyes glittered like diamonds as more memories emerged from the shadows of the past.

It was indeed an immense ballroom, as large as a cathedral. More people were working all around the walls, and on scaffolding right up to the ceiling, restoring the grandest murals I have ever seen, illuminated by banks of glaring floodlights.

The vast, original, unsupported ceiling had clearly been destroyed in the fire, and must have completely collapsed, because the splendid ornate tiled floor, though cleaned up, was chipped and pitted where masonry had fallen upon it as the upper floors fell through, and the new ceiling was currently mostly plain white plaster, upon which skilled artists were painstakingly recreating the colourful murals.

But I could see how spectacularly beautiful this room must have once been. Lacking, for now. the dripping gold of the other rooms, it had an elegance that was captivating. I could almost imagine a hundred women in lavish ball-gowns swirling around with their immaculately uniformed partners to the music of an orchestra.

I remembered sitting with Nan, long before this trip was even conceived, listening as she described glittering occasions in ballrooms like this, in the more carefree days of the monarchy. We would sit, in her kitchen with a cup of tea and a home-made scone in winter, or with a glass of wine in her pretty little garden in summer, talking about the wealthy and powerful from all over the world who had come to this palace and danced in this ballroom, watched from the side-lines by the young Natalie.

Suddenly she said "I once danced with a prince here."

I looked at her in amazement. "Really? I did not know that."

"Ah," she said, "I don't tell you everything," and grinned wickedly.

* * *

"Of course, I wasn't officially part of the royalty," Nan explained, "so I shouldn't even have been there. But Alexandra always allowed me to attend and watch, and one of the girls would lend me a gown. On this occasion, just before my sixteenth birthday, we were here for a grand dinner and ball. I was standing over there, near the windows, when a young man walked up to me, bowed, and

235

asked me to dance. He was about my age ~ a little older, perhaps, but not much ~ and my height, very good looking, with neat blonde hair and a shadow of a moustache under his nose. He wore a dark blue military dress uniform, which suited him very well.

"I was stunned and embarrassed, and looked quickly around me in case he was really addressing someone else, but there was no-one nearby. I stammered that I was not royalty, just a Lady in Waiting, and he smiled and said that it didn't matter to him, I was the most beautiful girl there, and he wanted to dance with me. So we danced; it was a magical moment, like a dream come true.

"He said his name was Frederick, and he was from Sweden. His father was a duke of some kind, close to the Swedish royal family. I told him my name, and as the dance ended, he asked if he may write to me; of course I said yes. He walked me back to where he had first spoken to me, and we found two vacant chairs and sat for a little while talking. But his mother suddenly arrived and, with a glare at me, told him to return to his family. Then he was gone, and I sat alone again in my little corner, floating on a cloud."

She was beaming, and I felt so close to her and so proud I could feel tears in the corners of my eyes. "Oh Nan," was all I could say as I hugged her.

Sergey politely waited until we were ready, then informed us that most of the remainder of the palace was closed off, as extensive rebuilding was still under way. We could see more, he said, but there would be little to interest us, as work was only just beginning, and some parts were too dangerous to open up. He said that the authorities hoped this would one day be a national museum, fully restored to its original splendour, but that they expected it to take many years.

236

So, by common agreement, we left Catherine Palace and rejoined our driver, who hastily discarded a cigarette as we approached (eliciting a frown from Sergey). He opened our doors for us, then took his seat and drove us the short distance to our real destination.

~ Alexander Palace ~

Alexander Palace, when we reached it after a short drive across the park, was certainly not as large, or as grand, as its sister that we had just left, but impressive in its own way. It, too, was damaged, but not by fire ~ it had clearly been neglected for many years.

The car slowly circled an oval, grassy island, overgrown with wild summer flowers and sprawling shrubs, then stopped beside the central entrance. A pair of bronze athletes reared above us in frozen motion on either side of a short flight of wide, stone steps, flanked by two rows of Roman style columns.

Absent-mindedly, Nan ran her fingers over the pendant of her necklace as she gazed at the Palace. She seemed afraid to go any further, to even get out of the car. I put my hand on her arm and leaned close. "Are you ok?"

She nodded, and I studied her face. Her eyes were still the same warm hazel, and her pale skin was still remarkably smooth, but her hair, once black, was now pure white, and where it had once flowed lustrously down to her shoulders, was now neatly permed. The combination of its colour and shape made the effect of a halo, and she looked for all the world like an angel.

Slowly we stepped out onto the gravel drive. It was hard to suppress a shudder of excitement. In this building had lived the supreme (some said despotic) rulers of Russia, in astonishing luxury, and for a small part of that time, my Nan had been there, close to the family.

I looked around. Above us towered a colonnade of white pillars, stretching right and left, the width of the centre span of the building, topped by an ornate balustrade.

Behind the collumns, a broad formal garden, laid out with pools and flower beds and chequered marble walkways, led to the palace doors. There was a sad sense of neglect about the whole place, paint was peeling, gutters broken, weeds filling every space, and I could see that part of the right wing was badly damaged by rainwater and mould.

But the thing that struck me most was the colour of it all. I had only seen black and white photos in books from the library, dating back to the palace's glory years, and had half expected it to be in shades of grey. But, of course, it wasn't. What I saw that day took my breath away. The façade of the palace was painted a luxurious shade of warm umber ~ though flaking now, and smudged with mould and water-stains ~ measured with white window frames and dotted with golden embellishments. It was incredibly beautiful, not as ostentatious as the other palace, but designed to impress in a more restrained way, which it most certainly succeeded in doing.

Sergey accompanied us as we walked slowly the few paces from the car to the first of the wide steps, feeling the mid-day sun warm on our shoulders, smelling the sweet scent of the wild flowers, and hearing the soothing hum of bees as we made our careful way.

Nan could not walk fast. Her legs, which had served her so well in the past, were no longer reliable, and she leant on her sticks to steady herself, so we made slow progress to the entrance. I held her left arm lightly, more to reassure her than for support, and I noticed Sergey's hand hovering close to her right elbow in case she should stumble. She stopped several times to look pensively around, but her expression had become inscrutable.

We walked up the short flight of steps, between the two statues and the central pillars of the colonnade, and through the remains of a formal garden, up to the heavy, oak, central doors. There, the soldiers accompanying us had joined with others already present to form a small guard of honour for us.

The doors were open, and another Marine was standing just inside the doors, tall and handsome in his uniform. He was wearing his medals, perhaps in our honour, and they made an impressive row of colour on his chest. He surprised us by demanding to see our passports and visas.

Flustered, we rummaged in our bags and extracted them. When we passed them to him, he made a great and serious show of examining the documents, opening each, scrutinising the pages and comparing our faces the the photographs inside. Eventually, his part acted out to the full, he returned the documents to us and waved us through with a salute and, it must be said, a small, wry smile.

"The building is res-pon-si-bil-it-ay of the Navy," explained Sergey. "But not use now. This, too, is be repair one day."

We stood in a spacious entrance hall, roughly square, with a parquet floor beneath our feet and a heavy chandelier hanging at its centre above our heads.

Another room was visible opposite, through marble columns, and that one was a mournful sight. Daylight was shining from above like a spotlight onto a massive pile of timber and rubble that lay at the centre of the floor. We walked towards it, stepping carefully over debris that had spilled out into the entrance hall. As we stopped between the pillars at the edge of the room, our feet crunched on some broken glass, and we jumped as a flock of pigeons flapped suddenly from the debris, disturbed by our arrival, and flew up and out of the shattered roof.

We could now see that the ceiling had completely collapsed. Broken glass and plaster were scattered all around; there was a smell of decay, and the dust raised by the departing birds rose in clouds that swirled in the daggers of sunlight. Poking from the heart of the debris was the skeleton of a chandelier.

"This was the Semi-circular Hall," Nan informed me as we surveyed the ruin before us. "The family held banquets in here ~ three or four-hundred guests at a time." She looked upwards and pointed with her stick. "It had a domed roof and a painted ceiling, and that chandelier used to hang down from the centre of it, like the one behind us."

The two side walls of the room held a row of tall windows, every pane smashed, while the far wall opened through broken French doors onto an overgrown boulevard of tall, slender trees. Standing in the midst of the remains, it was possible to feel the weight of centuries of history, of monarchs, good and bad, loved and hated, who had enjoyed enormous privileges there. But now it just looked incredibly shabby and neglected.

"The palace was left empty from 1918, after the family left," Nan told me. "The victorious revolutionary army closed it up. They removed all the treasures, which had become the 'property of the people'."

I nodded. I knew from my research that the building was allowed to gradually fall into disrepair, finally suffering a battering by shells and bombs as the German army advanced into Russia during the Second World War.

* * *

We stood and stared for a while, then Nan turned decisively back to face the entrance. There, keeping a respectful distance, to allow Nan the freedom of her memories, we found Sergey and, beyond him, the starched sentry at the doors. Off to our left, as we now faced it, was an opening leading into what was regarded, in its time, as the 'public' wing, where guests stayed, or were entertained.

But we turned to the doorway on our right, into the 'English' wing, where the family used to live. It took us into a vestibule or ante-room, with a door opposite and two flights of stairs to our right ~ one going up, and one down.

"Down there is the basement," Nan commented, pointing, as we paused to look. "The other stairs go up to the children's rooms and the staff accommodation."

With Sergey still trailing we continued, passing through one room after another, each bare, with only a hint of the luxury of the past in their mahogany panelling or intricate parquet floors.

Nan showed me where the Tsar's rooms had been, and we lingered for a moment in his private office. I had seen photographs of him standing in this very office, smart and erect in full military uniform, beside an enormous oak desk, with thick rugs on the floor and pictures of past monarchs on the walls. Now it was bare and cold and coated with dust.

"Nicholas was seen as a weak leader with bad judgement," said Nan, as though reading my mind. "He certainly let too many people do things in his name, including Alexandra. And as for the generals, they blamed all their military failings on him. After the thwarted 1905 revolution, he was persuaded to start the Dumas, a kind of parliament, so the people had some illusion of a say in the government. But they were not fooled, they wanted control, revolution, to overthrow the monarchy completely."

* * *

We moved on, and reached a bright room, with a bay window at the far end. There were shredded rags of curtains through which shafts of early afternoon sun lit a haze of floating dust, and revealed boxes and broken furniture strewn haphazardly around. Empty shelves along two walls showed that it had once been a library.

"This is one of the small libraries," Nan told me. "This is where I used to work on the day's correspondence with Tatiana. We were in here on the day that changed all our lives forever, when we received the news that Nicholas had abdicated, and that started the chain of terrible events that ended with their deaths. Tatiana and I were sitting over there, at a table near the window, when her mother called for her to tell her about the abdication."

She was quiet for a while, deep in her thoughts, looking around the room, seeing ghosts.

"Are you all right?" I asked.

She nodded, sadly, "I have realised that it is a mistake to try to relive the past, it can never be the same."

"You only have to do as much as you want to, you know" I said.

She hugged me. "Thank you dear, I'm fine. It has just been rather a shock to see it all in such a state."

Then she seemed to gather herself. "Shall I show you where my rooms were?"

I nodded, still more concerned about her welfare, and we walked along a corridor between Nicholas's rooms until we reached a rear staircase. "There are lifts between all the floors," she explained, "Nicholas had them installed when the family moved here from the Winter Palace. They wouldn't work now, of course, there is no electricity. This stairway was used by the staff to reach Alexandra's or Nicholas's quarters."

"Ladies, please," Sergey interrupted, anxiously, as we were about to mount the first step.

I had forgotten for a moment that he was still with us.

"It is not good. If you are fall, I am trouble."

"Sergey, darling," Nan replied, "I have travelled

hundreds of miles for this. I understand your concern, but I will not be put off."

He looked sad and worried, but said no more.

We started up the stairs, treading carefully in the almost total darkness, guided by a faint light ahead. Some of the steps creaked ominously, but they felt firm enough underfoot, until about we reached a huge hole where they had collapsed completely. Something heavy had fallen from somewhere above and taken the stairs on its way through. The glow we had seen was light seeping down from windows in the floor above us.

There was no way onward, so we turned back and retraced our steps through the Tsar's rooms, back to the stairs near the entrance hall that we had passed on our way in. These were more substantial, stone steps, dusty, but safe.

At the top, we turned left and then right, stirring up eddies of dust as we moved, with poor Sergey following glumly a few paces behind. Our way was lit, though barely, by sunlight threading through holes in the ceiling where the roof had weakened, allowing water to leak in and damage the plaster. Eventually, Nan led us into a straight, empty corridor. On the left and right at regular intervals were doorways, though all the doors appeared to be either open or missing or hanging at strange angles.

"This," she said, softly, "is where the maid's quarters were."

We walked a few steps and looked into the first doorway on our left, which led to the shared bathroom.

The senior maids, Nan told me, took turns to have a hot bath each day; supposedly according to a rota based upon their order of precedence, but it was frequently overridden by necessity. After them, the junior maids got in when they could.

The walls and floor were tiled a hideous green, and a white, cast-iron bath, with ornate, gold-painted feet, still stood in the centre of the room. There was a radiator and a bulbous Dutch stove against one wall, and a pedestal wash basin on another wall. A small window, high in the remaining wall, gave a little light.

Continuing along the corridor, we reached the next doorway. This accessed a small apartment that, Nan informed me, belonged to Elizabeth Ersberg, one of the Empress's personal maids. Elizabeth had come to Russia with Alexandra from Germany when the royal couple were married. Through the broken door that hung drunkenly across the entrance, we could see into the distressed bedroom beyond. It was bare, but for debris from a roof fall that was scattered over the floor.

Slowly, we proceeded to the third doorway. There, Nan stopped and turned to me, afraid for a moment to look. I heard Sergey clump to a halt behind us.

"These were my rooms" she said, and I noticed real nervousness in her voice and saw anxiety on her face. "I was given my own suite when Tatiana made me her Lady-in-Waiting. Before that, I shared with Rada and Polya, in a room further down the corridor, there." She pointed. "But, although it was a great privilege to have my own rooms, I missed the company, and spent as much time as I could with the twins in their room."

The door was open, but she still hesitated, as though afraid of what she would find inside, then, with an air of determination, walked in, then paused to wait for me

We stood in a small entrance vestibule, with a dusty maroon velvet wall covering, which hung in shreds. A door to the right revealed a tiny wash-room, with a small pedestal basin, while another doorway, straight ahead, led to the bedroom.

Amazingly, her bed was still there: a beautifull, brass, four-poster, now covered with dust and debris, and broken in half by a huge piece of timber that had fallen from the roof and lay across it. As we edged carefully into the room, I tried to imagine it as she had known it, bright and comfortable. I tried to see the young Natalie, asleep in that bed, but the present, with its dust and rubble, was too pervasive. The remains of lace and velvet curtains sagged and trailed downwards over the bed like rags of clothing on an ancient skeleton. A small table with carved legs was laying, crushed, on the floor beside the bed, with the pieces of a decorated porcelain wash jug and bowl scattered around it. There was a small window to our left, the glass broken, which looked out, past the colonnaded palace entrance, over the parkland surrounding the palace. Wires hung from the ceiling where there had once been a light fitting. It all smelt musty, with a hint of burnt wood from somewhere.

We stood in silence for several minutes, then she whispered "Elizabeth, I would like to leave now, please."

I looked at her face, and her eyes were filled with tears. "This was a mistake," she said sadly. "I should have kept my memories; they may not have all been good, but they had colour and life. Now I shall remember only this, the crushed bones of what my life once was."

We retraced our steps, down the stairs and out to the car. She did not speak again as we took our seats and the car moved off, but I could see that her mind was busy. Her lips would twitch or press tightly together, her eyebrows raise, as thoughts occurred and were processed. I spoke to her once or twice, trying to assess her mood, but her answers were vague. I feared that she was again sinking into depression.

She broke the silence when we were once again

speeding along the motorway. With a smile, she suddenly turned to me and said: "I met him again in London, you know ~ Frederick, my Swedish Prince ..."

~ Not The End ~

Natalie Tereshchenko ~ Lady In Waiting

~~~~

Russia, a country shrouded in secrecy, staggering under an oppressive, warmongering ruler ~ while the citizens die of cold and starvation, the royal family lives in opulence. But revolution is in the air, and things are about to change.

Although Natalie Tereshchenko works for Tatiana, second eldest of the daughters of Nicholas II and the Empress Alexandra, she is no ordinary Lady In Waiting ~ she is a niece of the Tsar himself, but it is a secret that no-one will admit.

As the Russian monarchy collapses, Natalie travels with them into exile, revealing her own insecurities and longings, her friendships, the men who loved her and the one who deceived her. When the family is slaughtered, she discovers that she cannot escape her past, and is driven to make an agonising decision.

~~~~

The **Tapestry Capricorn** books
for young teens of all ages ...

Tapestry Capricorn, Feline Secret Agent

~~~~

When undesirables start to flood across the dimensional boundary into Earth, a special agent is sent to deal with them. But an agent alone, even a shape-shifting cat, sometimes needs an assistant or two. Tapestry Capricorn enlists a bunch of unlikely allies to help her destroy the portal and send the rats back to their home world.

Reptilla

~~~~

Suddenly, it all becomes deadly serious.
Once again Tapestry Capricorn is called upon to deal with dangerous, dimension-crossing aliens. This time she faces an army of humanoid reptiles, led by a megalomaniacal lizard calling himself King Sah-Seh-Sah of Reptilla. With only a small white dog called Kong to help her, is she out of her depth this time?

~~~~

Printed in Great Britain
by Amazon.co.uk, Ltd.,
Marston Gate.